Ernenwein, Lesli

Mystery raider /
Leslie Ernenwein

LP

D0419136

MYSTERY RAIDER

MYSTERY RAIDER

LESLIE ERNENWEIN

WHEELER
CHIVERS

This Large Print edition is published by Wheeler Publishing, Waterville, Maine, USA and by BBC Audiobooks Ltd, Bath, England.
Wheeler Publishing, a part of Gale, Cengage Learning.
Copyright © 1953 by Leslie Ernenwein. Copyright © renewed 1981 by the Estate of Leslie Ernenwein.
The moral right of the author has been asserted.

LIBRARY OF CONGRESS CATALOGING-IN-PUBLICATION DATA

Ernenwein, Leslie.
   Mystery raider / by Leslie Ernenwein.
     p. cm. — (Wheeler publishing large print western)
   ISBN-13: 978-1-59722-694-3 (pbk. : alk. paper)
   ISBN-10: 1-59722-694-7 (pbk. : alk. paper)
   1. Large type books. I. Title.
PS3555.R58M97 2008
813'.54—dc22   2007044814

BRITISH LIBRARY CATALOGUING-IN-PUBLICATION DATA AVAILABLE

Published in 2008 in the U.S. by arrangement with Golden West Literary Agency.
Published in 2008 in the U.K. by arrangement with Golden West Literary Agency.

U.K. Hardcover: 978 1 405 64416 7 (Chivers Large Print)
U.K. Softcover: 978 1 405 64417 4 (Camden Large Print)

Printed in the United States of America
1 2 3 4 5 6 7 12 11 10 09 08

MYSTERY RAIDER

CHAPTER ONE

Morning's sun poured its scorching shine across the towering barricade of the Gilas; it ran brassy bright through Telegraph Pass and flooded the long flats where Yuma town retained the constant heat of a hundred sun-punished days. It climbed the Territorial Prison's east wall and turned the cell blocks into stifling, foul-stenched ovens. But because this was the day Jim Maiben had been waiting for, he ignored the heat. With deliberate care he drew a cross on the side wall of his cell and said, "The last one."

There were over a thousand crosses on the wall; a mark for each day Jim Maiben had spent in Yuma Prison. "Three years," he muttered, and tossed his pencil into the slop bucket.

Those years had left their mark on Jim Maiben. They had turned his smoke-blue eyes bitter and bleak; they had shaped his angular face into an inexpressive mask, so that he appeared older than his twenty-eight years. But his long body, broad through the shoulders and narrow at the hips, was straight as a buggy whip. Most prisoners resented work on the rock pile; sulking like barn-soured horses they swung their single-jacks with ineffectual slowness. But not Maiben. Hard physical labor at the rock pile had been his only haven from the awful pressure of thinking, and it had kept his muscles hard and his limbs supple.

His willingness to work, and his unfailing obedience, had been a source of much conversation among the guards. They were wary of him at first; familiar with various types of convicts, they'd been unable to classify him. By the look of his frowning face and the rank tone of his voice he appeared to be a tough one — a go-to-hell con who would cause trouble. "A candidate for the Snake Den," was how Yard Captain Drake tallied him.

Afterward, as the weeks went by and Maiben neither disobeyed the rules nor fraternized with fellow convicts, they decided he was a loner, hating all humanity. That opinion was verified when, during an influx of new prisoners, Captain Drake asked Maiben if he would like a cellmate and Maiben said flatly, "Not if I have a choice."

In all the three years of confinement no man had made friends with him, nor had he asked a favor from a guard. Now, as Maiben listened intently for the solid tromp of Yard Captain Drake coming to unlock his cell, a tight-coiled expectancy gripped him. Standing at the double gates of his cell he grasped a bar in each hand.

Why didn't Drake come?

Why make a man wait on the day his time was up?

Drake always escorted out-bound convicts on their last march to the warden's office. It was part of the routine, as unchanging as the heat and the stench and the flavorless food; part of the awful sameness that made each day seem like a week. Part of the caged monotony that rubbed the thin coating of human integrity from a man so that, in time, he thought and felt and acted like an animal.

Jim Maiben revealed no sign of the eagerness that clawed him now. He waited in the quiet desperation that had become his habit. A man learned to mask his feelings in prison; he learned to hide his hatred and nourish it against the time of reckoning. . . .

The convict in a cell across the corridor asked, "Ain't this gitaway day for you, *amigo?*"

Maiben nodded, feeling no kinship for Joe Franz or for any man in this place. He listened to footsteps coming down the corridor, recognizing the slow shuffle of Father Michael's *huaraches*. The old priest, whom the convicts called Father Mike, had visited him many times, fingering his ivory crucifix and talking about the futility of hatred.

"Good morning, son," the priest greeted. "You should be very happy this day."

Maiben shrugged. "I'm not out of here yet," he muttered.

"But you soon will be. And may God go with you, step by step, as you travel to a new life."

"Being free is all I need. Just freedom."

Father Mike nodded. "Exactly," he agreed. "But leaving this prison won't make you free. You've built another prison that holds you tight — a prison of hatred. There'll be no real freedom until you cast off the shackles of hate you've worn so long."

Maiben gave his attention to shaping a cigarette. What, he wondered, did this old priest know about hate? Father Mike hadn't stood in a courtroom and heard a jury sentence him to prison for a crime he hadn't committed. . . .

"I investigated your case many months

10

ago," Father Mike said. "Wanting to know all the facts, I journeyed to Tonto Bend, talked to Sheriff Sid Bishop and others. They told me you were a member of a group which set up an arbitrary deadline against new settlers in the Barricade Hills."

"Did they tell you that those settlers butchered my steers when they needed beef for their tables?" Maiben asked cynically. "Did they tell about the irrigation dam that dried up the south fork of Commissary Creek?"

Father Mike shook his head. "They told me that you were seen near a house which was burned, and that you'd had trouble with the owner. They said the prosecution made an air-tight case of arson against you."

As if repeating a denial made distasteful by long usage, Maiben said flatly, "I didn't burn Ike Fenton's shack. Sure, I hated his guts, and I wanted to run him out of the country. But I wasn't near his place the day it was burned."

The old priest eyed him for a moment before saying, "I believe you, son. And I'm deeply grieved that you were unjustly accused. But there's no reason to hate the men who convicted you on such seemingly sound evidence. If they erred it was an honest mistake."

11

"A mistake that cost me three years of my life," Maiben said harshly. "A mistake that shouldn't happen to a dog." Then he asked, "What makes you so sure I hate those men?"

"You've shown it in many ways," the priest explained. "Refusing my counsel, and the friendship of your fellow prisoners, you have built a prison within a prison, and lived in it alone, month after month. Other men have been placed in solitary confinement as punishment. But you, a model prisoner, chose to suffer the punishment of aloneness. Hatred did that to you, son, and it can harm you even more after you leave here. Hate is contrary to every truth the Bible teaches us. It is sinful and destructive. Won't you let me help you unlock your personal prison?"

Maiben took a deep drag on his cigarette. He said, "Look, padre. I'm willing to admit you're right, according to the Bible. But that doesn't change what's inside me. Nothing can change that. I'm going back to Rampage Basin and pay off for what they did to me."

"Don't do it, son," Father Mike pleaded. "Don't keep yourself a prisoner of hatred. Forgive those you believe have trespassed against you."

"Including the dirty dog whose lies sent me here?" Maiben demanded.

"Yes," Father Mike urged. "Forgive him and be free."

Maiben laughed at him. He said rankly, "I'll forgive the bastard with a bullet between his eyes."

Father Michael sighed. He stood there for a moment longer, as if reluctant to admit defeat. Then he said, "I'm sorry for you," and walked slowly along the corridor.

Maiben flipped his cigarette into the bucket. He paced the nine-foot cell, taking three steps and turning in the methodical march he had tromped so many times. When he came back to the cell gate Joe Franz asked, "You got enough cash for the trip to Rampage Basin?"

"Yes," Maiben said. "It's in the locker room along with my clothes and gun."

Then, as if becoming aware of Franz's intrusion into his personal affairs, Maiben asked, "What business is it of yours?"

"Just wondered, is all," Franz said, revealing no resentment. "I've got a few dollars I won't be usin' for a long, long time. Thought you might need a loan."

Maiben shook his head. "Haven't got much, but I won't need much," he muttered.

As if relishing a fond memory, Franz said, "You should stop off in Tucson and see

13

them swivel-rumped gals at Lulu Kane's place. They sure make a man feel young and frisky." He sighed, and said regretfully, "That's the worst part of this place. No women."

But Jim Maiben wasn't listening. He was watching Yard Captain Drake come along the corridor. . . .

The big man unlocked Maiben's gate. He said, "Come on, cowpoke. Warden Stone wants to kiss you good-by."

Maiben followed him, remembering all the times he had visualized this last march from the cellblock. Now that he was actually walking out it didn't seem quite real. He thought, This is it. A few minutes from now I'll be free! But it still didn't seem real.

The lifer in Number 9 cell said, "Good luck, and don't come back."

Maiben handed him a nearly full sack of Durham; he gave a farewell salute to each man at a gate as he passed, and for the first time felt sorry for all of them. . . .

"Don't forgit what I said about them gals at Lulu Kane's place," Joe Franz called after him.

"Git staggerin' drunk tonight," another convict suggested.

And another called, "Tell the gals in Tucson I'm bein' true to them."

A hoot of derisive laughter ran along the corridor. It settled into a harsh-toned yammering that slowly faded as Maiben followed Drake across the sun-scorched quadrangle toward the administration building. He looked back once, and thought bitterly, Three years.

A long time, in jail. A hellish long time. But not long enough to forget Tonto Bend. The town was like a magnet, pulling at him, drawing him with an irresistible force that couldn't be denied. Thinking back to his trial, and what had preceded it, Maiben recalled those courtroom faces with a fresh clarity. There was the blandly smiling face of Clyde Hatabelle, the lying land agent whose testimony had convinced the jury; the eager confidence of his North Fork enemies, and the shamed faces of men he'd thought were his friends.

Again, as he had so many times, Maiben silently cursed the four cowmen who had seemed to share his fight against Hatabelle's rag-tag settlers. One of them had burned Ike Fenton's sorry shack and let him take the blame for it. All of them had deserted him when the chips were down.

But clearest of all those courtroom memories was the face of the girl he had wanted to marry. That, somehow, had been the worst part of it for Jim Maiben, the most surprising and disgusting. Dulcie Todd had seemed to believe his story. But it shouldn't have made any difference to her, one way or the other, considering how it was between them. Guilty or innocent, she should have been for him a hundred per cent, and that's how she seemed to be. Visiting him at the jail every day, Dulcie had brought nicknacks from the hotel where she worked as waitress. She had reached through the bars to hug him the day of his trial and said confidently, "The jury won't convict you, Jim."

But the jury did, and that had been too much for Dulcie Todd. Maiben grimaced, recalling the last time he had seen her — the day she gave him back his engagement ring. "Three years is such a long time to wait," Dulcie had explained.

So long to wait.

She hadn't said anything about how long those years would be for him. Not a goddamn word. She just stood there outside the jail cell, waiting for him to say something, and when he didn't, she asked poutingly, "Well, aren't you going to say anything?"

There'd been just one thing he could say. He said, "Go to hell!" and pitched the ring into a cuspidor.

Three years ago. Yet even now, after a thousand days in Yuma Prison, he hadn't been able to discard the memory of her ripe lips. *Kissing* lips, he'd called them when he first started courting her. Nor had he forgotten how she'd snuggled in his arms and whispered, "Jim, honey." A man had too much time for remembering in prison, especially at night when sleep wouldn't come. He could remember how soft and white and smooth her flesh was, and the feel of her arched back in his hands as she pressed against him. And the woman smell of her . . .

"You don't look much pleasured, for a man that's on his way out," Captain Drake complained.

Maiben shrugged, retaining the strict silence which had kept him out of trouble for three years. Going into Warden Stone's office he stood without visible sign of emotion.

The warden's farewell speech was brief. "You've been a good prisoner," he said, mopping his bald head with a soggy bandanna. "Try being a good citizen, and you'll have no more trouble."

Seeing the cynical smile that quirked Maiben's lips, Stone asked, "Still think you were railroaded?"

Maiben nodded.

"Well, the law makes a mistake occasionally," Stone admitted. "But it's done with now, and you'd best forget it."

Maiben thought, Forget hell! How could a man forget three years in this stinking place? Three years of sweating and waiting and eating slop fit only for hogs. Three years without climbing into a saddle, or roping a steer, or being with a woman; a thousand nights of caged-up misery with the walls closing in so tightly you seemed to be suffocating. How could a man forget that? Maiben felt like shouting his derision, but he shrugged, knowing how useless it would be.

"Revenge won't give you back the time you've served," Stone warned, "and it might mean another stretch in here."

Maiben walked to the door and opened it before saying, "Next time I'll be guilty, Warden. Guilty as hell."

He was thinking about that when the locker-room clerk returned his belongings.

"This gun could stand some oil," the clerk said, handing over a Walker-model Colt. Peering at the dusty, unmarked weapon, he said jokingly, "My, my. Not a single notch."

"There will be," Maiben promised. "It may take a little time, but there'll be one."

CHAPTER TWO

He rode out of Yuma town shortly after noon, ignoring the advice of a well-meaning liveryman who'd sold him a horse and saddle. "Better wait till sundown," the man had said. "You'll be cooked to a blister before you top Telegraph Pass."

But a savage eagerness was in Jim Maiben — the pent-up impatience of a man who'd waited long to make this ride. The livery-stable proprietor couldn't know how good it felt to be asaddle; how fine it was to tilt the brim of a battered old Stetson against the bite of noonday sun — to go where he pleased when he pleased, with no goddamn walls to hold him back. Men didn't sit in saddles up there on the Hill, nor wear Stetson hats, nor feel the welcome weight of a loaded gun in a half-breed holster.

Maiben felt like laughing. He opened his mouth and tried to laugh, but it wasn't much more than a chuckle. When he tried it a second time the result was even less like laughter. He thought, I've forgotten how to laugh, by God! and was shocked by that knowledge.

But he was free.

Free as a scalawag steer hightailing over a ridge.

Keeping his bay gelding to a steady trot, Maiben calculated the time it would take him to reach Rampage Basin. By cutting south of Antelope Hill stage station and going through the Tinajas Altas country he might make it in four days.

It took five. . . .

He rimmed West Divide on the fifth day with afternoon's long shadows slanting across the Barricade Hills. From this high, bald crest he glimpsed the remote glint of his sun-silvered windmill on the mesquite flat where his adobe house stood. Beyond that and to the north was another windmill, barely visible in the far-off heat haze — Bart Volpert's place. To the south, where the dry fork of Commissary Creek angled through dun-colored hills, were the ranches of Alamo Rand, Ernie Wade, and Red Pomeroy, all hidden by the intervening bulge of timbered ridges.

"Looks about the same," Maiben mused, scanning the vast scattering of hills and the valleys between them. A trifle more dry, perhaps, but good cow country. Yet he felt no excitement, none of the soaring satisfaction a man should feel at coming back after long absence. The thought came to Maiben that he wasn't seeing this country as a rancher returning to home range, but as an ex-convict seeking revenge. That was what three years in Yuma had done to him.

Maiben started down the slope, then stopped abruptly as his eyes caught a metallic glint off to the left; a brief flash as if sunlight had been reflected from metal. From a rifle barrel, perhaps, or a silver-plated bit shank. For upward of five minutes he peered across the brush-fringed crest of rimrock, expecting to see a rider. But there was no sign of movement, and the flash didn't show again. Why, he wondered, would anyone be riding the rim? No cattle climbed this high, for there was nothing up here but rock and buckbrush.

Shrugging off his troubled thoughts, Maiben rode down the long slope and into timber. The aromatic scent of pine needles reminded him of the times he had hunted for deer late in the fall when beef roundup was over and a man got a hankering for venison. There was a big mesquite thicket on the South Fork where wild turkeys wintered; fat young toms that made good eating along about Thanksgiving time. Good country, these Barricade Hills. Or it had been, until Clyde Hatabelle messed things up with his goddamn plowjockeys. . . .

Maiben identified Bart Volpert's Spade brand on five cows, only two of which had calves, and Red Pomeroy's Three Bars brand on a steer. Presently, as he approached Spanish Spring's shallow, rockbordered seep, he saw two of his Roman Six cows and one with Ernie Wade's Running W, none of which had calves.

Dismounting at the spring, Maiben got down on his belly and drank cheek to cheek with the bay. Because the desert's parched heat had sucked him dry, he remained there in the hoof-pocked mud, absorbing its welcome wetness and thinking about the plan he had decided upon months ago in Yuma. There wasn't much chance of discovering the dirty son who had burned Ike Fenton's shack and let him take the blame, or of making Clyde Hatabelle confess that he had lied in court. The land agent was a thoroughly stubborn man. An ambitious man, also. He wouldn't give in to threats; might not even talk under pressure of brutal punishment.. But he could die, and the man who killed him could cross the Mexican border in the dark of one night's riding. After that it would be a case of waiting until the bank sold his place and sent him whatever was realized over the mortgage against it. Banker George Jessop would take care of that. He was, Maiben thought now, his one real friend in Rampage Basin.

There seemed no need for him to stop by at his adobe house; nothing there he wanted. Tonto Bend was his destination, and Clyde Hatabelle his target. Yet Maiben felt an oddly insistent urge to spend one night under his own roof. He was thinking about that when a voice called from the boulders above him: "Stand up — and don't touch that gun!"

A woman's voice . . .

Maiben remained motionless for a moment of bewildered disbelief. What would a woman be doing here?

"Get on your feet," she commanded.

Maiben obeyed and saw her standing in a cleft of rock above the spring. Her face, beneath the brim of a shapeless gray hat, was like a golden mask in the fading sunlight; an oval, full-lipped mask with high cheekbones and the bluest eyes he had ever seen. Maiben was urgently aware of the pistol in her hand, but it was this woman's face, framed in tawny sorrel hair, that most strongly attracted his attention. Perhaps it was because he hadn't been this close to a woman for so long, or just the unexpectedness of her being here, but the sight of her almost took his breath away.

"Who are you?" he asked.

She ignored his question, not speaking as she came down slowly, leading a saddled horse. Maiben met her probing inspection with an appraisal equally deliberate. Young, he thought; not more than twenty-two or three. She wore denim riding pants that revealed shapely thighs, and a man's cotton shirt that seemed too large for her except across the bosom. It fitted snugly there. He had thought at first that she was the prettiest woman he had ever seen, but now, observing her at closer range, he understood that she was not pretty in the way Dulcie Todd was, or the others he'd considered to be pretty. It was something more than that. Handsome, perhaps, or even beautiful. But not pretty.

The pistol she held was aimed at his midriff. Maiben wondered if it was loaded, and supposed it was. She had the hammer thumbed part way back, which was dangerous if her thumb happened to be moist with perspiration. She didn't look nervous, though; in fact she seemed calm as a queen stepping down from a throne, and as confident. But there was no telling about a female with a gun in her hand. . . .

"Why you aiming that at me?" Maiben asked quietly, not wanting to excite her.

She halted close to him, her appraisal continuing for another long moment before she asked, "What are you doing here?"

A cynical grin slanted Maiben's beard-stubbled cheeks. He said, "I could ask you the same question."

"Where'd you come from?"

"Off the Tinajas Altas."

She flicked a glance at the bay's hip. The strange brand seemed to convince her, for she lowered the pistol and said, "I mistook you for someone else."

"Is that why you stayed out of sight up on the rim?" Maiben asked, remembering the metallic glint he had seen.

"I wasn't up there," she said.

The casual, almost disdainful tone of her voice whipped up a wicked flame of resentment in Jim Maiben. Who in hell did she think she was, pointing a gun at a man on his own land — ordering him around as if he were some lousy saddle bum looking for a handout? It occurred to him now that he had left this country three years ago smart-

25

ing from one woman's rejection; now another woman welcomed him back with a gun. . . .

"You play a trifle rough," he suggested.

There was no change in the cool serenity of her eyes as she said, "Well, I'm sorry if I frightened you." But she didn't sound sorry, and the disdainful expression remained.

"I've been worse scared and lived," Maiben muttered. Then he took a quick step forward, wrenched the down-tilted gun from her hand, and tossed it aside.

"Why, you miserable sneak!" she exclaimed.

Maiben watched anger warm her eyes and stain her cheeks. She didn't look cool and serene now; she looked like a passionate, hot-eyed woman. It was an odd thing, but in this fleeting moment Maiben thought, Like a woman who's just been kissed. And although there was no resemblance except that they were both females, she reminded him of Dulcie Todd.

"Pick up that gun," she commanded.

Maiben laughed at her. And then, acting upon pure impulse, he reached out and took her in his arms.

"Take your dirty hands off me!" she protested, struggling to pull free. Her hat fell back to hang by its throat thong and her tawny hair came down in wild disorder. The feminine scent of her was like a delicate perfume, intimate and tantalizing. And her lips, so red and moist and sweetly curved, were an invitation that overwhelmed him. . . .

"Don't you dare!" she cried, and getting one hand free, clawed his cheek from ear to chin.

Maiben captured the hand and drew her against him. She was still struggling, still panting like a hot-eyed dancer when he kissed her.

Abruptly, as if there was some potent magic in the merging of their lips, she ceased struggling. For a moment she was inert, neither rejecting nor responding, her body a cushioned softness in his arms, then she kissed him with a pressing eagerness that astonished Jim Maiben.

It was like a wave, that kiss; a high-cresting wave that broke abruptly as she pulled her mouth away, exclaiming, "Don't — please don't!"

Maiben released her. It was coming dusk now and he couldn't identify her exact expression. But her voice held a breathless pleading. "Don't what?" he asked.

"Don't kiss me again."

Maiben thought about that as she rearranged her hair, and was baffled as a man could be. In all the years of his bachelor-hood he had never forced his attentions on a woman. The fact that he had with this one astonished him. He'd thought Dulcie Todd had cured him of women. A fickle, flirty, selfish breed, he'd told himself; a teasing, trollopy breed that a man should leave alone. Yet he had kissed the first woman he met. . . .

Now, as she climbed into saddle, Maiben said, "Your pistol, ma'am." He picked up the gun, gave it to her.

Holstering the weapon, she peered at Maiben as if puzzled by this tall man in seep-mucked clothes; as if not quite sure about him and wanting to be sure. "Are you looking for a job?" she asked.

Maiben shook his head.

"So you're just a saddle tramp," she mused.

"Do you make a habit of kissing saddle tramps?" Maiben inquired.

She drew the back of a slim hand across her mouth as if wanting to wipe away a shameful memory. She said, "Damn you!" in an outraged voice and went past him, making an indistinct shape as she rode off at a gallop.

Maiben fingered his scratched cheek,

wondering who she was and why she had been gunning for someone. Someone who looked like him. He shrugged, not much caring, and said, "To hell with her." But he couldn't discard the impression she had made on him; couldn't help remembering how it was with her in his arms — how hugely her lips had roused him. He ran his tongue along his lower lip, savoring the wild sweet flavor of her lips.

What, he wondered, had caused her to return his kiss?

She had been angry as a woman could be, had clawed his face like a spitting cat. Angry and proud. Proud as a queen. Yet for one brief moment she had been open and receptive as a parlor-house girl.

"Women!" he muttered, smearing the word with contempt. They were all alike, all trollops at heart. Some put on airs and acted like ladies, but there was a sprawly streak in the best of them. Remembering how much Dulcie Todd had meant to him, and how easily she had discarded him, Maiben was disgusted with himself. A man should learn some sense after a deal like that, should know enough to stay away from females. He shook his head, not understanding it at all. He thought, I went for her like a mare-chasing stud, as if I'd never seen a woman before.

Kneeling at the spring, he took a long, leisurely drink of the lukewarm water. Seemed like he couldn't get enough of it after the hot ride across the Tinajas Altas. He had thought there was nothing he needed at his place, but now he understood there was one thing — a long, soaking bath in the windmill water tank.

"Maybe I'll spend the night in it," he mused.

Picking up the bay's reins, Maiben got into saddle. He was turning away from the spring when a bullet whanged past his head, that snarl of sound merging with a rifle's sharp report on the timbered slope behind him.

Maiben clawed instinctively for his gun; he whirled the bay in a pivoting turn toward a protecting rock outcrop. But in this same moment the rifle blasted again and a bullet slashed across Maiben's left shoulder. He fell from saddle, holding to one rein; he grunted and lay motionless on the dusk-veiled ground.

Who in hell was shooting at him? he thought. Not the girl, for she had ridden off in the opposite direction. And she had no rifle.

For what seemed an intolerably long

interval there was no sound save the bay's gusty breathing. Maiben remained on his belly and peered upslope at the dark belt of timber. Did the dry gulcher think him dead, or was the dirty bastard playing it cautious? Again Maiben wondered who had fired at him, and why.

The wound in his shoulder had sent darting slivers of pain across his back when he struck the ground. Now it settled into a dull ache, and he was aware of the wetness of blood dribbling below his left armpit. Anger built up in Maiben until it was a swelling pressure. That sneaky son up there hadn't missed killing him by much. Except for the fact that he'd been turning away from the spring the bullet would've drilled straight through him instead of slicing across his shoulder.

Maiben cursed softly, thought, What a hell of a welcome home!

This country must've gone haywire for a fact. First a female threatened to gut-shoot him with a pistol; now some bastard was shooting at him with a rifle. Maiben tried to guess who the bushwhacker might be, and could think of no one except Clyde Hatabelle. The land agent might have found out the exact time of his release from prison, and that he was coming horseback instead of by stage. Perhaps Hatabelle, fearing what a vengeance-seeking ex-convict might do, had decided to get in the first shot. But even so, it wasn't like him to wait with a gun. The land agent had always done his fighting in a law court. He was that kind of dude.

"Unless he's changed in the past three years," Maiben reflected aloud.

It occurred to him now that his assailant had evidently followed him down from the rim, so the woman had told the truth about not being up there. And she had mistaken him for someone else. Not for Hatabelle, who had yellow hair and was half a head shorter.

Then, from an old accumulation of suspicion, came the thought that it might have been Red Pomeroy. Red was tall and lean-bellied; the carroty color of his hair wouldn't show from a distance. Was it Pomeroy she'd been gunning for, and who had shot at him?

All this in the tense interval while Maiben listened for sound of movement on the slope above him. It was dark now, with only a slight afterglow remaining. The thought came to Maiben that his assailant might be sneaking toward him afoot, wanting to get in a shot at close quarters. With that threat prodding him, Maiben glanced up at the vague shape of his horse, watched the bay's ears.

The gelding heard something. His ears were pricked forward!

Maiben held his gun ready for instant firing. He probed the yonder darkness. If that self-winding polecat wanted a shootout. . . .

Then Maiben heard it, too — a remote tromp of hoofs crossing rocky ground, and presently there was the rhythmic beat of a loping horse, that sound soon fading.

"Gone yonderly," Maiben muttered, and stood up.

Why had the dry gulcher backed off? Did he believe he'd scored a kill, or was he too cautious to find out?

Afterward, riding slowly along a cattle trail toward his place, Maiben remembered that there was another man who might have waited for him on the rim: Ike Fenton, the settler whose shack had been burned three years ago. The nester had built his sorry shack during roundup when all five ranchers were busy gathering beef. By the time they discovered his presence, Fenton had a homestead claim established.

Maiben cursed, remembering that he had wanted to run Fenton off at once. But Bart Volpert, arguing against such violence, had influenced Rand, Wade, and Pomeroy into cautious waiting. Better to starve Fenton out, Volpert had counseled, revealing no resentment when Maiben accused him of being a chicken-livered coward. For that's what it had amounted to, in Maiben's opinion. Fenton had talked fight, warning that Clyde Hatabelle and the law courts were behind him. But the homesteader was bluffing, and after that he slow-elked a yearling whenever he needed beef for his table. . . .

Traveling at a walk through this night's mealy darkness. Maiben wondered if he should go on to town without stopping at his house. The wound didn't seem to be bleeding now, but there should be a bandage to protect it against infection. Fingering his scratched cheek, he thought, Two wounds, and wondered about the woman who had used her fingernails on him. She had seemed so calm and coldly aloof, so self-contained — until he kissed her. Then, for a fleeting moment, she had been the direct opposite. Like a woman in love.

"Odd," Maiben mused, not understanding it at all.

But that bafflement was mild compared to what he felt upon skirting a mesquite thicket just west of his adobe house. Wholly astonished, Maiben peered at the doorway lamplight that made a yellow beacon across the yard.

Someone was living in his house!

CHAPTER THREE

Maiben pulled up the bay. He stared at his lamplit house with swift-rising resentment. Who would have the gall to take over his place like this? Observing a high-wheeled hay rake in the yard he thought angrily, Some goddamn nester!

So aroused that he forgot about his wounded shoulder, Maiben rode into the yard at a run. This, he told himself, was the last straw. On top of what had happened at Spanish Spring, it was too damned much. As he slid the bay to a dust-boiling stop a woman came to the doorway — the woman with sorrel hair. She wore an apron now, and instead of a pistol, she held a skillet in her hand.

"Oh, so it's you again," she said, quite casually.

She made a tall and womanly shape standing there with lamplight behind her; a shape that disrupted the orderly run of Jim Maiben's thinking.

"Is there something you want?" she inquired after a moment.

As it had been at the spring, her voice was low and throaty, revealing no excitement, no fear. The thought came to Maiben that there was something else in it: an undertone of sadness, or regret. But what in God's name was she doing here?

By what possible authority had she decorated the windows of his house with those frilly curtains?

"You live here?" Maiben demanded.

That seemed to surprise her, for she peered at him as if wondering about his mentality. Standing so, with one eyebrow arched higher than the other, she looked like a school teacher peering at a stupid pupil.

Resenting her attitude, Maiben said rankly, "Don't look at me like I'm a thumb-sucking dunce."

"Then don't ask such stupid questions," she retorted.

"Stupid? I asked if you lived here. What's stupid about that?"

"Well, it seems pretty plain that I'm living here, doesn't it?"

Maiben shook his head. "Not to me, it don't."

"This is the Eric Steffan ranch," she announced, "and I am his daughter."

"So?" Maiben mused, wholly baffled. "And you?"

"Name of Jim," he said. He was on the point of giving his last name when a man called from inside the house: "Who is it, Gail?"

"A stranger named Jim."

"Well, ask him to take pot luck with us," the man suggested in a voice rich with Swedish accent.

That didn't seem to please her, and for a moment Maiben thought she would reject her father's suggestion. Then she said, "Supper will be on by the time you put up your horse."

A cynical, self-mocking smile slanted Maiben's cheeks. This, by God, was loco as a drunkard's dream, him being invited to eat supper in his own house. "Don't mind if I do," he said, and rode toward the corral.

Gail Steffan was a trifle uppity for a nester's daughter, Maiben decided. She needed whittling down to size. He grinned, thinking now that he had kissed one of Clyde Hatabelle's emigrants; one of the ragtag bunch Hatabelle called "agriculturists." A few of them might be honest farmers. But mostly they were a shiftless, thieving breed wanting to crowd out their betters. Give them a toehold and they'd take over the whole range. And they'd ruin it with their plowing and their hoeing. In five years' time they would turn it into a grassless desert of drifting dust. He had seen it happen in Texas. First there'd be only two or three sodbusters, then four or five. But they kept coming, and they kept crowding until they gobbled up all the grass. Like this Steffan woman and her father, taking over his house.

Well, she wouldn't be so uppity when he told her this was his place and he didn't cotton to nesters living on it. Maiben chuckled, thinking how surprised she'd be. Might teach her not to call the next stranger she met a saddle tramp. . . .

He unsaddled, and because there were three horses in the corral, tied the bay outside. No use taking a chance on getting his pony kicked by a nester's plow horse. He forked it a feed of hay from a stack that smelled freshly mowed; walking toward the house he felt a warm wetness on his back, and thought, It's started bleeding again.

Presently, as Maiben washed at the basin on the front stoop, Eric Steffan hobbled to the doorway on crutches. He was a tall, gray-thatched Viking of a man with the same kind of high cheekbones and blue eyes as his daughter, the same prideful serenity. "Good evening," he greeted. "I did not hear your last name."

"Didn't give it," Maiben muttered.

Wiping his face on the roller towel, he observed the suspicion that came into Steffan's eyes, and the speculative way the old man glanced at his half-breed holster. Steffan, he guessed, was regretting his invitation. And after supper, when he got ordered off the place, Steffan would regret it even more.

The old man absently fingered his down-swirling mustache; he asked, "You have ridden far?"

"Far enough."

Steffan made a slow, clumsy turn on his crutches and said, "Supper is on the table."

The smell of home-cooked food was a fine thing after three years of prison slop; it made Maiben's mouth water as he sat down at the table. He asked, "You lived here long?"

"Almost seven months," Steffan said. He glanced at his right leg, which was stuck out stiffly to one side. "The last three weeks seem longer than all the rest."

"Leg broken?"

Steffan nodded.

They ate in silence for a time, Maiben tackling his generously piled plate with a hungry man's relish. Eating my own beef, he thought amusedly. It seemed fantastic that he should be sitting here with these two people, where he had eaten so many suppers alone. And the room was different. There were scalloped paper borders on the shelves, a rocker sat on a round hooked rug beyond the stove, and a floor-to-ceiling drape partitioned off the sleeping quarters at the west end. It seemed more orderly and more cheerful; it reminded him of a poem he'd once read about the way a woman's fingers could contrive to turn a house into a home.

That was what Gail Steffan had done to this long room — made it seem homelike. But she had no right here, Maiben reminded himself. Nor did her old man. You would think they expected to remain permanently, the way they acted. Like they owned it. Nesters were usually pretty meek, and pretty shiftless, but not these two. Glancing at Gail Steffan, who sat across the table from him, Maiben found her watching him. He wondered what was behind the calm and inexpressive face she showed him at this moment. Was it indifference, or secret speculation? Or the masked dislike of a woman resenting an impulsive kiss?

Her lamplit hair, so thick and lustrous, shone like burnished copper as she got up and took the coffeepot from the stove. After refilling his cup, she stood for a moment, peering at his blood-stained shirt. Then, as if reluctant to believe it, she asked, "Can it be that you've been shot?"

Maiben nodded, and now Eric Steffan exclaimed, "Shot! Why did you not tell us?"

"Bullet creased me, is all."

Gail went to the stove and poured hot water into a pan, then took a clean dish towel from a shelf. "Take off your shirt and I'll wash the wound," she offered.

"Don't bother," Maiben said, wanting no favors from her.

"But your shirt is so dirty," she insisted. "There's danger of infection."

While Maiben considered that counsel, she said, "Don't be bashful. I have seen men's bare backs before."

"Who said anything about being bashful?" Maiben demanded.

This woman had a way of making a man feel stupid. And he disliked accepting favors from a female nester who was going to be kicked off the place. But he thought, She's right about the danger of infection. As he unbuttoned his shirt, Steffan asked him,

"Where did this happen?"

"Spanish Spring."

The old man thought about that for a moment before saying, "That is where I was shot, which seems a strange thing."

"I thought you had a broken leg."

"Broken by a bullet, while I was laying pipe near Spanish Spring."

"Pipe? For what?"

"A water line to the north forty," Steffan explained. He smiled in the way of a man seeing land that pleased him. He said, "That would make a good fenced pasture, if it had water. A fine place to finish beef steers for market."

Maiben nodded, remembering that he'd had the same idea when he first came here, and that George Jessop had agreed to loan him money for pipe when the mortgage was paid off. But why should a nester go in for such improvements on someone else's land? And what did Bart Volpert think about it?

"Volpert wouldn't like it being fenced," Maiben suggested. "Quite a few of his cattle use that for a crossing to Spanish Spring."

"Which is why I'm on crutches, most likely," Steffan said.

That didn't make sense to Maiben. Bart Volpert was too much of a gentle Annie to get mixed up in a shooting scrape. Spade's owner might threaten a lawsuit, but he was against violence in all forms. The man was a physical coward, to Maiben's way of thinking. . . .

"What would you being shot have to do with Volpert?" he asked, wincing a trifle as Gail used disinfectant on his wound.

Steffan shrugged. "I did not see the man who fired at me. But Bart Volpert tried to buy this place the same week I came here, and he has not been neighborly toward us."

"But he wouldn't shoot you," Maiben said, very confident about this. "If you'd squatted in his front dooryard he wouldn't use a gun against you. It must've been somebody else."

Steffan peered at him with a sharper attention. "You know Bart Volpert?"

Maiben nodded.

"And you are his friend?"

"Well, not exactly. I know him, is all."

"Then you have been in Rampage Basin before," Steffan mused, stroking his mustache in the absent fashion of a man considering information that might have significance.

Maiben asked, "Is Ike Fenton still squatting on Pantano Flats?"

Steffan shook his head. "There is no one by that name living around here now."

"Well, there's a couple men in these hills who might shoot at a nester," Maiben suggested.

"But I am not a nester," Steffan objected.

Maiben peered at him, holding his arm up for the bandage Gail was fashioning around his wounded shoulder. What in hell was Steffan trying to put over? Did the old man think that possession of a place for seven months amounted to ownership?

Steffan smiled at him as if amused. "So you took me for a nester," he said. And glancing at Gail, he asked, "Do we appear that poor, daughter — as if we could not buy land?"

"You mean you own this place?" Maiben demanded, his voice sharp.

"Of course. It is not all paid for yet. But I have bought this ranch and it is mine."

Maiben absorbed that announcement in shocked silence. The words "not all paid for" rang a bell in his mind. George Jessop must have sold him out. Perhaps the bank had got caught short of cash, or Effie Jessop had talked her husband into liquidating a mortgage that was long past due. But Maiben couldn't quite believe it. George had told him not to worry about the mortgage while he was in prison. "Forget it," he had said. "I'll send somebody out there from time to time to take care of things until you get back."

"Who did you buy it from?" Maiben asked.

"The Tonto Bend Bank," Steffan said. "I have heard that it was taken from a man named Maiben who was sent to jail."

Finished with the bandage, Gail brought him one of her father's shirts. "I'll wash yours and mend it," she offered.

Accepting the shirt, and remembering what he had intended to do, Maiben felt more ashamed at this moment than he had ever felt. He was the trespasser here, not her. He was what she had called him: a saddle tramp. Hell, even the shirt he was putting on was borrowed.

He said, "Thank you, ma'am."

"You're welcome," she acknowledged, and now the sound of a rig wheeling into the yard sent her to the doorway. She stepped out on the stoop as if she'd expected the caller, and Maiben heard her say, "We have company. A drifter named Jim."

Maiben had hung his gun gear on the back of his chair; now, as he strapped it around his waist, he said to Steffan, "Much obliged for the meal. Guess I was pretty hungry."

"You are more than welcome," Steffan

46

said graciously. "Sleep in the barn tonight, if you wish."

"Well, thanks."

As Maiben picked up his hat, Steffan asked, "Would you be interested in a job, just for a week or two? Until I'm able to work. My daughter has tried to take care of the place, but it is man's work and there is much that needs doing."

"Well, I'm not exactly looking for a job," Maiben said, searching for some polite way to tell this old man he had no time for odd jobs.

"A friend has promised to help," Steffan said, nodding toward the doorway. "He will start getting in the hay tomorrow morning. But he is a busy man, and if you would help him, the work would not take so long."

Maiben became aware of a man's voice outside; the voice seemed familiar. He was trying to identify it when Gail came in followed by a yellow-haired, blandly smiling man who took one look at him and ceased smiling.

Maiben said, "Hatabelle," in a voice that was like a sighing curse. He stepped around the table, both fists cocked; he said rankly, "I've waited three long years for this."

Hat in hand, Clyde Hatabelle stood in the doorway as if shocked beyond the power of movement. His scholarly, smooth-shaven face turned pale; in the lamplight he looked like a man stricken by some sudden illness. He said nervously, "I didn't know you had come back."

"You know it now," Maiben muttered. "Put up your hands and fight!"

"No," Hatabelle protested. "I have — there's no reason for it."

He was like that, wide open as a man could be, when Maiben pitched forward and struck him viciously in the face.

The land agent fell back against the doorframe. He swung an ineffectual fist that glanced off Maiben's thrusting arm; he backtracked to the stoop, dropping his hat and yelling, "No, Maiben — no!"

Remotely, as if it came from a far distance, Maiben heard Eric Steffan's voice demanding, "Is his name Maiben?"

Hatabelle was backing off the stoop when Maiben hit him in the face again, and then slugged him with a sledging right to the belly. Hatabelle loosed an agonized grunt; he staggered backward, and at this instant, as Maiben followed him off the stoop, a gun blasted from somewhere across the yard.

The bullet splintered the doorframe against which Maiben had been standing. The sound of it yanked him around and he shouted, "Put out that lamp!"

He had his gun drawn and was crouching in the deep shadow alongside the front wall when the house went dark.

CHAPTER FOUR

For a tense interval there was only the sound of Clyde Hatabelle's labored breathing. The land agent was down, by the sound of it, and Maiben thought, That last one hurt him.

Scanning the dark yard, Maiben wondered who had fired the shot. There was no doubt in his mind about whom the bullet was meant for; a split second before the shot came he had been framed in the doorway, a lamplit target the bullet had barely missed.

It occurred to Maiben now that it must be the same man who had done the shooting at Spanish Spring. The dry gulcher had circled and come here for a second try. But what was behind it? What reason could anyone have for shooting at a man who'd been away from the area for three years?

From the open window behind him came Eric Steffan's low voice asking, "Do you see anyone?"

"Keep away from the window," Maiben warned.

There was no telling when that bastard would open fire again. And he didn't seem worried about hitting a woman; that slug of his might have hit Gail instead of the doorframe. . . .

Guessing that the hidden gunman might be near the barn, Maiben stepped over Hatabelle and cat-footed around the house. Moving quickly now, he skirted the rear wall, and coming to the corner nearest the barn, stood listening.

For a seemingly endless interval he heard no sound save the bay gelding methodically munching hay over by the corral. Thought of Hatabelle out front made Maiben impatient. He'd had the land agent on the run, so near collapse that one good punch might have put him out completely. That, somehow, seemed damned important. To knock him cold. After that, when Hatabelle regained consciousness, he could try making him confess to the lies he'd told the jury. But first he had to knock him out. Maiben grinned, thinking about it; he rubbed the bruised knuckles of his left hand against his pants leg. Many a night in Yuma Prison he had visualized how it would be, feeling Hatabelle's flesh against his knuckles. It was just as he'd imagined; it had put a thrusting gladness in him and the fine hot glow of it had made him tingle all over, like being with a woman. Clyde hadn't liked the punishment; he'd yelped like a kicked dog. And he'll yelp some more before I'm through with him, Maiben thought savagely.

Something attracted his attention — not a sound, exactly. For a moment, as he probed the yard's west side, he couldn't understand what it was that had pulled at his attention. Then, abruptly he knew: his horse had stopped munching hay.

That must mean that someone was moving over there, yet Maiben saw no sign of it. Nor did he hear anything for another long moment. Then, as one of the horses in the corral nickered, Maiben's eyes picked up movement south of the barn. There was no moon, and very little starlight; all he glimpsed was an obscure shadow moving against the night's quilted darkness.

Maiben fired, and side-stepping instantly, waited for a blob of muzzle flare to target. But instead of shooting, the rider spurred his horse into a run. Maiben sent two more bullets in the direction of that sound, then listened to the diminishing rumor of hoofbeats.

Who was it? Why was he gunning for an

52

ex-convict — for a man who no longer owned an acre of ground?

By God, there was no rhyme nor reason to it!

Recalling that Alamo Rand had been his nearest neighbor to the south, Maiben tried to think of some reason why Rand would want him out of the way, and could think of none. Alamo, who had a wife and three small children, hadn't acted very friendly after the shack-burning, but there'd never been any trouble between them.

The mystery of it baffled Jim Maiben, and angered him. How could you fight a man who fired from ambush and then ran off like a spooked jackrabbit? If the bastard wanted to kill him so badly why didn't he stay and shoot it out? The sneaky son had come close to killing him twice. There was a limit to how far a man's luck would stretch with that kind of stuff. The third try might well be successful. . . .

Maiben heard the tromp of hoofs out in the front yard. For a moment he couldn't understand what it meant; then, as the sound of wheels crunching gravel came to him, he understood that Hatabelle was making a hasty departure.

"Another spooky one," Maiben muttered, and hurrying toward the corral, he observed that the lamp in the house had been lighted. Hatabelle, he calculated, could be overtaken within two or three miles. A dude land agent in a buggy couldn't outrun a man on horseback. Maiben was hoisting his saddle to the bay's back when Gail Steffan came across the yard and asked, "Where are you going?"

"After Hatabelle."

"But haven't you hurt him enough?"

"He was able to get up, wasn't he?"

For a moment she just stood there looking at him. Then she asked, "You mean you intend to kill him just like that?"

Maiben nodded.

"Because he testified against you?"

"Because he lied."

"No," Gail said, very urgent about this. "Clyde wouldn't lie."

Maiben laughed at her, mirthless, sardonic laughter. He said, "So you've got a case on the handsome land agent."

"He has asked me to marry him," she said simply. "Why do you hate him so?"

"He testified in court to seeing me leave Ike Fenton's burning shack," Maiben said. "I wasn't within five miles of the place that day."

"But Clyde believed he saw you," Gail insisted. "He must have. Clyde wouldn't lie about a thing as important as that."

Maiben shrugged and reached for the saddle's cinch.

"Even if it wasn't you, Clyde didn't lie about it," she said. "Can't you see the difference?"

And when he ignored that question, Gail continued thoughtfully, "I mistook you for someone else at Spanish Spring today. Perhaps Clyde made the same mistake that I did."

"A damned costly mistake," Maiben muttered, and yanked the cinch tight. "A mistake I intend to pay him for, the only way it can be paid."

He was picking up the bay's reins when Gail said, "I think Clyde mistook you for the same one who fired that shot a few minutes ago."

"Who?" Maiben demanded.

Eric Steffan called from the stoop: "I would like a word with you, Jim Maiben!"

Ignoring that summons, Maiben asked again, "Who?"

"Come talk to Dad, and I'll tell you," Gail offered.

Her face was faintly revealed by the long shaft of doorway lamplight. She was now as she had been the first time he saw her at Spanish Spring — proud and serene and self-reliant. Her blue eyes, calmly watching him, held the same appraising speculation. But because he had once felt the response of her lips, Maiben understood that behind this shield of aloofness lurked a brimming well of emotion; a hunger and a love of life she couldn't wholly suppress. Remembering its brief revelation at the spring, he thought, All woman.

Her offer to name his assailant whetted Maiben's curiosity; it fashioned a wedge of indecision in him. She might know something, or she might be stalling for time. . . .

"You trying to give Hatabelle a longer head start?" he asked bluntly.

She nodded. "A trade of time, for information."

That frank admission surprised Jim Maiben and pleased him. Here, by God, was a woman who said what she meant, and meant what she said. It seemed ironic that she should be slated to marry a muffin-mouthed land agent — a yellow-haired liar who talked in circles.

"You've made a deal," Maiben said. Looping the bay's reins around a corral post, he accompanied her to the house.

Eric Steffan was puzzled as a man could be. He sat in the rocker with his game leg propped on an overturned bucket and watched Jim Maiben place the lamp on the floor so that its light was diminished.

"Do you think there might be another attack tonight?" Steffan asked.

Maiben shrugged. "No telling about a dry gulcher," he muttered.

"I cannot understand it," Steffan said, the gravity of his voice matching the deep frown on his age-mottled face. "It makes no sense to me at all. I thought the trouble was caused by friends of yours, resenting that I had bought your ranch. Clyde warned us that it would be worse when you came back from prison. He said you might try to scare me off this place. But how is it that you also are being shot at?"

"Can't figure it out," Maiben admitted. He took a chair at one side of the doorway and canted his head, warily listening for sound of movement in the yard. "Must be one of Hatabelle's loco nesters who had a hunch what day I'd get back. Those plow jockeys on the North Fork don't like me much."

"But why would a nester shoot at me?" Steffan asked, glancing at his bandaged leg. "I have given them no trouble. There has been no bad feeling between us. Yet I, too, was fired upon."

Maiben shrugged and shaped up a cigarette. Feeling uneasy, he went out and slowly circled the house, taking time to listen at frequent intervals. This, he thought, was how it would be for him from now on; night or day he would be listening and watching, always knowing that he'd be shot at again. Until he found the man who was gunning for him. . . .

When he went back into the house and sat down, Steffan said, "We were strangers in Tonto Bend and knew nothing of what had happened before we came to this country. I want you to know that I bought this place in good faith."

Maiben shrugged and watched Gail stir up the fire. She moved the big coffeepot to the front of the stove, her face an obscure oval in the shadows there. All her movements, he observed, were graceful; she had a smooth, unhurried way of doing things, an agility and a suppleness that hugely attracted him.

As if taking time to choose the right words, Steffan said thoughtfully, "It is too bad you lost your ranch. Even though you are a single man, it is too bad."

"Did George Jessop mention the fact that he promised to hold off on my mortgage until I got out of jail?" Maiben asked.

"I never saw Mister Jessop. I dealt with his widow, who had taken over the bank sometime before."

Maiben revealed his surprise in the way he said, "So that's how it happened. George died." A cynical smile slanted his cheeks as he added, "I got sold out by a woman — again." He took a long drag on his cigarette and exhaled the smoke slowly. "Effie Jessop and Dulcie Todd. Damn them both."

But Maiben felt better about it, and showed that shift of feeling by saying, "I should've known George wouldn't sell me out." He grinned, thinking back. "We used to go deer hunting together, weeks at a time. Effie Jessop didn't like that. She said George should be attending to business instead of traipsing off into the hills with a man who owed the bank money. Old George was one friend who stuck by me through thick and thin."

Watching him now, Gall Steffan marveled at the change in Maiben's angular face. There was a kindliness and a tolerance there that astonished her. At this moment it seemed impossible that he was the scowling, hard-eyed tough who had used his fists so savagely on Clyde Hatabelle.

Eric Steffan seemed to share that surprise too, for he asked, "Then you do not resent having your place sold?"

Maiben shook his head. "It was no fault

of yours, or of George Jessop's. Perhaps Effie didn't know about George's promise to me. But it wouldn't have made any difference to a woman."

"Your opinion of women isn't very high, is it?" Gail suggested quietly.

"It couldn't be lower," Maiben said.

Gail saw the old bitterness come back into his eyes as he added harshly, "The real fault is Clyde Hatabelle and his lying testimony."

"Clyde lie?" Eric Steffan asked, wholly puzzled. "Do you believe Clyde is a liar?"

"He lied me into Yuma Prison."

"Ah, that I will not believe," Steffan objected, emphasizing the rejection by holding up both callused palms. "There is no more honorable man in Rampage Basin than Clyde Hatabelle." He glanced at Gail, silently asking affirmation and getting it in an obedient nod of her head.

Maiben smiled, thinking that these two people looked alike and thought alike. Their kinship was something more than that of father and daughter; it was an alliance of two calm and resolute individuals who shared a mutual integrity. . . .

"Clyde is for the settlers," Steffan said. "But he has been fair with me, and I am a cowman."

Maiben shrugged. "Hatabelle has a knack

of making folks think he's a lily-white angel. That's why his testimony convicted me. It never occurred to the jury that he was lying."

"But he wasn't," Gail insisted. "Can't you get it through your head? Clyde must have mistaken you for another man."

"Then you don't think I burned Fenton's shack?" Maiben asked slyly, thinking he had trapped her.

"Not if you say you didn't," she said, meeting his gaze directly.

She was unlike any woman Jim Maiben had ever known. She talked straight, like a man. And she thought straight. She could look a man in the eyes, frank and open as a honky-tonk hustler sizing up a customer, and yet not seem brazen.

He said with grudging respect, "Well, thanks. Everyone else in this country believed your boy friend when he said he saw me leave that burning shack."

"I believe you both," Gail said. "I think Clyde saw a tall, black-haired man who looks like you from a distance."

Masking his curiosity, Maiben said, "Didn't know I had a double."

"You haven't really. He is older than you, and not good-looking at all. In fact his face is somewhat ugly."

That didn't make sense to Jim Maiben. What kind of damned foolishness was she handing him now? "The man looks like me but he doesn't look like me. What's his name?"

"Bart Volpert."

Maiben loosed a hoot of jeering laughter. "That," he announced, "is the best joke I've heard in years!"

"What's so comical about it?" she demanded.

"Well, in the first place, it was Volpert who refused my idea of running Fenton off. Bart is a gentle Annie; he's like your friend Clyde. A smooth talker who doesn't like rough stuff. He'll scheme and squirm, but he won't fight. Volpert talked Rand, Wade, and Pomeroy out of putting the boots to Fenton. Said it wouldn't be legal."

"Yet I've been told that he bought Fenton out for a paltry sum after you — after Fenton's shack was burned," Gail said.

That information surprised Maiben. But it didn't alter his opinion of Volpert, or weaken his argument. "Just proves what I told you. He's a schemer, not a fighter."

"Then if Volpert isn't doing the shooting, who is?" Steffan asked.

Maiben had no answer for that. Nor did another hour of talking, and two cups of coffee, bring an inkling of whom his assailant might be. But afterward, spreading his blanket in the barn, Maiben understood that Gail Steffan had accomplished something he hadn't thought possible: She had won a week of grace for Clyde Hatabelle. . . .

CHAPTER FIVE

The sign was plain. A man had ridden up behind the barn, dismounted, and led his horse to an old mesquite tree. There he had waited long enough to discard three cigarette butts.

Jim Maiben peered at the house, which was tinted by first sunlight, and calculated the distance to its bullet-splintered doorframe as being upward of a hundred yards. He studied the boot tracks, observing their size and shape; he picked up a mesquite twig and measured a boot mark exactly, using his pocket knife to notch dimensions. After that he followed a set of hoof prints that angled off southward, locating the exact point at which the horse had broken into a run.

Why, he wondered, hadn't the man fired back when shot at?

You'd think the bastard was short of ammunition; that he was conserving bullets.

Maiben stood there for a long moment, attempting to guess who his assailant was, seeking a definite clue to go on. Recalling Gail's notion that the ambusher was Bart Volpert, Maiben grinned. That was a woman for you, picking the one man in Rampage Basin who'd never been known to draw a gun against another human being. If that was an example of women's intuition, they could keep it.

A fragile blue tendril of smoke was rising from the stovepipe when Maiben walked back to the yard. Presently, as he led his horse to the windmill water trough, Gail came out on the stoop and said, "Breakfast is ready."

She wore a flowered kimono that fitted snugly at the waist, revealing the swell of ample breasts. A vagrant strand of hair made a slender sorrel wing that curved across her right cheek, and her eyes were heavy-lidded with sleep. Yet even now, with hair unbrushed and appearing only half awake, she seemed to possess everything a man would want to see in a woman.

"Yes, ma'am," Maiben acknowledged, and tried to take his eyes off her, and couldn't until she turned back into the house. Three years in Yuma, he thought, must've turned me soft. A man who had been bamboozled by a woman shouldn't get romantic notions about the next one he met. Especially an ex-convict without a pot to his name. But that reasoning didn't diminish the sense of anticipation in him, or change the tantalizing picture she had made standing in the doorway.

No wonder Clyde Hatabelle had offered to help with the haying. The thought of sharing a marriage bed with Gail Steffan would make a man willing to do most anything. He wondered if the land agent would show up this morning after the beating he'd taken, and guessed Hatabelle wouldn't. Clyde might need a couple days to recover. . . .

The kitchen end of the house seemed more cheerful than it ever had looked in the morning. It was odd, coming in here and being served breakfast by a woman. Odd, and hugely pleasant. No bacon had ever smelled so good, no coffee so fragrant, no egg yolks so golden. Aware of a delicate scent of perfume as Gail poured his coffee, Maiben compared this with the sour mornings at the prison commissary and thought, This is how it should be.

Observing that Gail had only a cup of coffee before her, he asked, "Aren't you eating anything?"

"I'll have breakfast later with Dad," she explained. "He dislikes eating alone. He says a man might as well be dead as to eat by himself."

Maiben nodded, understanding now what this house had always lacked; why it had been a cow camp instead of a home. A man could live here alone all his life and it would still be the same — a bachelor's cow camp.

"Dad didn't sleep well last night," Gail said.

"Leg ache him?"

"Yes, and he worries about things."

"And you worry about him," Maiben suggested, understanding the note of sadness he had detected in her voice last night.

She nodded. Lowering her voice to a confidential tone, she said, "The doctor thinks he may never ride again."

"Too bad," Maiben said, thinking now that trouble had a way of hitting the wrong people. Eric Steffan seemed such a fine old man; a kindly, honest man willing to work hard for what he got, and wanting no more than was due him.

"Dad worries about the bad feeling between cowmen and settlers," Gail said. "He sees no reason why there should be stealing and shooting in a country so big — where there is room for everyone."

"Sodbusters always make trouble," Maiben muttered. "They ruin whatever they touch, and they touch too damned much."

"But Clyde says his settlers are content to stay on the North Fork. What harm is there in that?"

"Ike Fenton didn't stay on the North Fork, and he caused me plenty of harm. Because of him, and Hatabelle, I spent three years in prison."

Gail poured him another cup of coffee. She said quietly, "I believe that most of Clyde's settlers are honest men who do not begrudge cowmen their grazing land. They are farmers, wanting flat land near water — not up here in the hills. The things they grow are good for Rampage Basin. Until they came, every potato and carrot and sack of barley sold in Tonto Bend had to be imported from somewhere else. Now we can buy those things cheaply, without paying high freight rates."

Maiben smiled at her. He said, "Hatabelle has done a good selling job on you." But because there was some merit to what she had told him, he added, "I'm not saying you're all wrong. But I'm not all wrong either."

"That's right," Gail said, expressing her pleasure in the way she smiled and nodded.

"It is the way Dad feels about it. He sees both sides of a thing and is willing to be fair."

Then gravity replaced her smile and she said, "But there is no fairness in what has happened to him. No chance for agreement. That is what worries him so much."

"Maybe I'll run down the dirty sneak who's worrying him," Maiben said. "The same one who's also worrying me."

"Oh, I hope you do," Gail said, very urgent about this. "I hope you have more success than Sheriff Bishop. He has done so much looking without finding a single clue."

"Did you tell him your suspicions about Volpert?"

She nodded and shrugged, saying, "Like you, the sheriff just laughed at me."

Afterward, as Maiben went out to his horse, Gail asked, "Will you come back?"

Maiben grinned at her. "Any reason why I should?"

Some secret thought stained her cheeks with color, so that for a moment she was like a blushing schoolgirl hearing her first romantic proposal. In this brief interval she seemed flustered by some secret knowledge. Then, as her composure returned, she said, "Yes, to bring back my father's shirt."

Maiben nodded, quite pleased that he had

69

pierced her shield of calm aloofness. She could be frank with a man and act as if he had never kissed her, but she couldn't think about the kiss without blushing. . . .

Now, as he rode out of the yard, Gail waved to him from the stoop and called, "Be careful, Jim."

That use of his first name hugely pleased Maiben. It gave him a fine sense of well-being. For the first time since leaving Yuma Prison he felt wholly free; not an ex-convict who'd been a number among other numbers, but a free man. Recalling Father Michael's counsel about the futility of hatred, Maiben had an inkling of what the old priest meant. During the past few moments he had forgotten there was a land agent named Clyde Hatabelle, or a debt of vengeance that should be paid. Perhaps a man's mind became so filled with hating that there wasn't room for anything else; for pleasant things like the intimate voice of a woman saying to be careful.

Following horse tracks southward, Maiben crossed the mesquite-dotted flats and climbed into a tumble of hills beyond them. He rode at a walk, scouting the thickets and rock outcroppings ahead with a constant vigilance. The ambusher had ridden directly south, making no attempt to circle, leaving a plain trail to follow. Considering this fact, and weighing its significance, Maiben wondered how far the man had gone. He might be up there on the next hill, waiting for a target. There was no telling about a dry gulcher. These tracks might be bait for the purpose of drawing a curious victim into a trap.

Maiben rode wide around an upthrust thickly screened by catclaw and ocotillo, crossed a lower bench of the hill, and picked up the tracks again in a dry wash. Half an hour later the trail petered out on a malpais slope; he spent upward of an hour tracing an occasional track through a wide scattering of porous, volcanic rock, then rode directly to Alamo Rand's ranch.

Rand, a round-faced, paunchy man in his late forties, was hitching a team to a buckboard. Dropping a trace chain, he exclaimed, "Well, Jim — so you got back!"

They shook hands then, and Maiben inquired about the other man's family. After that he asked, "What's been going on while I was away?"

"Plenty," Alamo said. "More'n aplenty." He leaned against a wheel and took out his Durham sack. Gravely, as a man reporting bad news, he said, "Never saw the beat of it, Jim. We've kept the settlers out of the

Barricades, but they're hurting us, regardless. Clyde Hatabelle claims they ain't doing no night-riding. He keeps saying they're all honest, God-fearing men and ain't the ones that's stealing us bankrupt. But we're being stole — and worse."

Rand glanced at his wife, who now came from the house with two little girls and a teen-aged boy. "It's gitting so this ain't a fit place for a family man, Jim."

Helen Rand came up to the wagon and said, "Why, it's Jim Maiben. I thought at first you were Bart Volpert."

That announcement startled Maiben. He asked, "Do you think I look like Volpert?"

"Why, no — you really don't," Helen said, embarrassment coloring her plump cheeks. "Mercy sakes, no. You're much better looking than Bart is, and a good ten years younger."

Then, as if eager to change the subject, she said to Alamo, "Hadn't we better be going? Lonnie's appointment with the eye doctor is for eleven o'clock."

Rand nodded, and finished hooking the trace chains. When he had handed the two little girls up to their mother, he said, "I've decided to sell out, Jim. Helen wants to leave here while we've got something to take with us."

"While I've got a husband who's not crippled," Helen Rand said emphatically. "Have you heard about Eric Steffan being shot?"

Maiben nodded, and Alamo said, "Somebody took a shot at me a week ago. In broad daylight, up near the divide when I was scouting some horse tracks that was made by a cow thief."

"I fret every time he goes riding," Helen Rand announced, "not knowing if he'll come back. It's got that hazardous."

"Make yourself to home," Alamo invited.

And his wife said, "Stay for supper if you'd like. You're more than welcome."

"Guess not, thank you kindly," Maiben said, and watched them drive off.

It seemed silly to search for a set of fresh horse tracks in this yard, but he rode a complete circle around the barn and corral, finding no sign of recent travel. The man who'd shot at him hadn't come here.

Afterward, riding toward Red Pomeroy's place, Maiben wondered who would buy Rand's ranch, and what price he was asking. Effie Jessop probably held some kind of mortgage on it, inherited from George. There was no way of guessing how much it amounted to, or if she would consider transferring the mortgage to an ex-convict who had no cash to pay down. One thing, though, he was reasonably sure of: Alamo Rand wasn't the one who had burned Fenton's shack. That, then, left Pomeroy, Wade, and Volpert.

Maiben shook his head; he thought, Not Volpert, and wondered about the other two. Ernie Wade had a wild streak in him, and went on a drinking spree occasionally. But he was short and stocky. Clyde Hatabelle wouldn't have mistaken him for a tall man — if the land agent had made a mistake.

Again, as on countless occasions during the past three years, Maiben's suspicion centered on Red Pomeroy. If one of the four Barricade Hills' ranchers had burned a nester's shack, Red seemed the most capable of doing it. He had disliked Fenton, and argued with Volpert about letting him stay on Pantano Flats.

Must've been Red, Maiben decided. But now, riding toward the showdown he had wanted so long, he felt no thrust of anticipation, no eagerness. He was puzzled that it should be so, that after all the months of waiting and wanting, he should feel no impatience now. What, he wondered, was wrong with him? Where was the itching eagerness that had plagued him during all those miserable months in Yuma?

A man should be licking his lips at a time like this. He ought to have his hackles up, ready for a wingding.

Day's heat increased, bringing out a smoky scent of dust and sun-cured grass and piney ridges. A lone buzzard wheeled high above a flat-topped mesa, riding the windless air on effortless wings; from some hidden canyon off to the west came the bawling of a cow, that plaintive sound flattening out against the far reach of open country. This was what Maiben had missed the most in prison — the sight and sound and smell of cattle range, the feel of big sky and big country. It was all familiar, and all good, until the thought came to him that he was no longer part of it.

"A landless saddle tramp," he muttered, and cursed morosely, thinking of the place he'd lost, the work and sweat and savings that had gone into it.

A man could lose a woman, and get along without her, or get himself another. Hell, the towns were crawling with chancey females if a man wanted a woman. But a good little ranch like Roman Six was hard to come by. Terribly hard. A man had to work for wages a long time, to get a start; he had to save and scrimp and go without a lot of things.

For the first time the full realization of his loss came to Jim Maiben. There had been too much excitement last night, and too much puzzlement. The knowledge that he'd lost his ranch had shocked him. But not like now, with an all-gone feeling in his stomach, so that he saw himself for what he was: an ex-convict who, at twenty-eight, possessed forty-odd dollars. A saddle bum in a borrowed shirt.

Even though he had intended to have Jessop sell the ranch for him after settling with Hatabelle, Maiben had taken it for granted there'd be enough money for him to make a fresh start somewhere else. In Sonora, maybe, or New Mexico. There were plenty of places where a man with a stake could start over again. But now he'd have to sign on with some cow outfit, working for wages — a round-up drifter chousing another man's cattle, riding another man's horses.

Maiben was savoring the bitterness of that understanding when he crossed the lower slope of a ridge and found Red Pomeroy unloading block salt from a wagon.

A pleased grin creased Pomeroy's perspiring, lantern-jawed face. He said, "Don't seem like three years, Jim," and came forward to shake hands.

"It does to me," Maiben announced,

drawing his gun and aiming it at Pomeroy's belt buckle. "It seems like thirty years."

The tall redhead teetered back on his heels. "What's this?" he demanded, and gawked in bug-eyed astonishment. "Why you pointing that gun at me?"

"Because you're a self-winding son-of-a-bitch!" Maiben raged. "By God, I should shoot you down without waiting for you to talk!"

"Talk?" Pomeroy asked. "What sort of talk?"

"You know damn well, and you'd better get it said fast."

The thought came to Maiben that Red looked astonished, and scared, but he didn't look guilty. . . .

"You must've gone loco," Pomeroy blurted. He backed up a step. He wiped his sweaty face on a shirt sleeve and said whisperingly, "Pure loco."

"Not so loco that I can't savvy who let me go to jail for burning Fenton's shack," Maiben announced.

"You mean you think I done it?"

Maiben nodded.

Red shook his head, plainly baffled. "I thought your talk about not burning the shack was just court talk, meant to convince a jury," he said. "You'd had a fist fight with

77

Ike, and argued with Bart Volpert about letting him stay. I thought sure you done it."

"You're a damned liar," Maiben accused rankly.

"I'm not lying," Red insisted. He nudged back his hat and used a finger to scoop beads of sweat off his forehead. "You mean someone else burned the shack and let you take the blame?"

"Yes," Maiben said. "You."

"But I didn't, Jim. Honest. Can't you see I ain't lying?" Red looked Maiben in the eye. He said, "You can kill me, but you can't make me admit doing something I didn't do."

Maiben eyed him for a long moment, not quite sure he was telling the truth, and knowing there was no way to be sure. He shrugged and lowered his gun and said, "Well, I had to try." Easing his horse off at an angle, Maiben kept the gun ready, not trusting Pomeroy's temper.

"No need to be spooky," Red assured. He loosed a gusty sigh and relaxed. "By God, you scared the hell out of me, Jim, bracing me like you did. I thought you'd gone haywire for sure. But I ain't blaming you for being suspicious, if you didn't burn Fenton's shack. I'd be the same way after three years in prison. I'd want to kill the bastard who was to blame." Then he added, "Light down and have a smoke."

The good-natured grin which accompanied the invitation convinced Jim Maiben. Holstering his gun, he dismounted and accepted the hand Pomeroy offered and said soberly, "I'm sorry for spooking you like I did. I had to find out."

Presently, as they squatted on their heels in the shade of a mesquite, Pomeroy asked, "You heard about Ernie Wade selling out to Bart Volpert?"

"Why'd he do that?"

"For the same reason Alamo Rand may do likewise — a worrying wife. Dulcie got scairt by all the trouble we been having."

"Dulcie? Did she marry Wade?"

Pomeroy nodded. "Right after you left. I thought you'd heard about it by now."

"Who'd tell me?" Maiben muttered. Remembering that he had mentioned Dulcie Todd's name in front of Gail, he wondered if she'd known whom he'd meant. Finally he asked, "What sort of trouble was Wade having?"

"Same as the rest of us. Calf-stealing, mostly. Never saw the like of it, Jim. They run off a steer for butchering beef, now and then, which is to be expected. But that ain't what's busting every outfit in the hills. It's the weanling calves that are being stole in bunches."

Maiben eyed Pomeroy in plain disbelief. "What would anybody want with weanling calves?" he demanded.

"Damned if I know. They're no good for beef, and they couldn't be drove far. But they're being stole. There's more bellerin' cows in these hills than you ever saw before in your life. Mother cows that's lost their calves. And it ain't just one ranch that's losing them — it's all of us. The thieves seem to take us in turn. Last month it was me. This month Bart Volpert has lost six or seven."

"Hasn't Sheriff Bishop come up with any clues?"

"None that's been worth a damn. He arrested a couple nesters on suspicion. But there wasn't enough evidence to convict them. It's the damnedest thing you ever saw, Jim. Them calves just disappear into thin air. Sid Bishop has rode his rump off, trying to trail 'em down. And so's the rest of us. But the tracks don't go nowhere. They just peter out."

Maiben thought about it, wholly mystified. Beef rustling was as old as the cattle business. A familiar part of it, in fact, for there'd always been a certain amount of loss from thieves. But never had he heard of wholesale calf-stealing. Hair-branding, yes. And so-called mavericking from the fringes of big outfits. Professional rustlers always concentrated on beef steers that could be moved fast and far and for which there was a ready market. Even when they ran off mother cows they seldom bothered with weanling calves, which slowed up the progress of a stolen bunch. . . .

"So that's why Ernie Wade sold out," Maiben mused.

"His wife talked him into taking the only offer he could get, which wasn't much."

"What would Volpert want with Wade's place?"

"Well, Bart seems to think that Hatabelle's settlers will take over this whole damn country in time," Red explained. "He says flat land will be selling by the acre five years from now."

"You believe that?"

"No, but I guess Ernie did. And Alamo Rand seems to favor the same notion. Least-wise his wife does."

Red grinned, adding, "That's how it is with family men. They do like their wife says."

"Where did the Wades go?" Maiben in-quired.

81

"Moved to town. Ernie tinkered around doing odd jobs for a spell, and then Dulcie took back her old job at the hotel. I guess Ernie should've stayed on a ranch. He used to space his sprees, but now he spends half his time in the Spur, guzzling bar likker. Seems like he's gone all to hell since Dulcie left him six months ago."

"So?" Maiben said, feeling no satisfaction at the thought that Dulcie had made a poor marriage, and wondering why he felt none.

"Maybe a man is better off single," Red suggested. "It gits downright lonely, sometimes. But he's his own boss."

Recalling that this redhead had once been sweet on Sheriff Bishop's daughter, Maiben said, "Thought you'd be hooked up by now."

"You mean Grace Bishop? Volpert married her two years ago."

"The hell he did!" Maiben exclaimed, and could scarcely believe it. "Didn't think Bart had any romance in him at all."

"Me neither," Red admitted. "He always acted like a natural-borned gelding that had no need for females. But he took Grace away from me easy as catching a hobbled horse." Red grimaced, revealing what that admission cost him; he said, "She was the only girl I ever wanted to marry. I can't abide bold women. Not for a wife. And there was nothing bold about Grace. She was that shy and nice it took me six months to even kiss her. I guess you just can't tell about women. One day they act like you're the only one, and the next day they're married to somebody else. Sure beats hell how women act."

"Yeah," Maiben agreed. "I found that out."

Presently, as he got into saddle, Maiben asked, "Did Volpert hire a man to put at Wade's place?"

"Well, yes and no. Bart dislikes to pay wages. He let the ranch rock along by itself for quite a spell. Then Burro Smith came back from Mexico, broke and hungry, so Bart put him on the place for his groceries."

Maiben smiled, recalling Burro Smith. He said, "I'll have to stop by and see the old hellion. He's the best shot with a rifle I ever saw, and the worst liar."

Afterward, angling eastward through the hills, Maiben wondered why the news of Volpert's marriage should seem important, one way or the other. Although Bart had never been less than amiable, they hadn't been friends or visiting neighbors. But now some half-formed thought nagged at Maiben's mind — something to do with Volpert's marriage.

CHAPTER SIX

Tonto Bend looked a trifle larger than Jim Maiben remembered it, with more houses and fewer vacant lots along the stage road at its west end. Riding down a dug-way to the bridge across Sabino Arroyo, Maiben recalled the last time he had heard hoofbeats bonging on these worn planks — the day Sheriff Sid Bishop had taken him to Yuma in the westbound stage. He had looked back at the town from the top of Apache Mesa, and observing that Bishop was watching him, had said, "Hope I never see the god-damn place again."

"You'll feel different three years from now," Bishop had predicted with an old man's wisdom. "You'll be glad to see it."

And so he was. . . .

Thinking of last night's fist fight, Maiben wondered if Clyde Hatabelle had complained about it to the sheriff. It would be like him to prefer charges of assault and battery against an ex-convict. Maiben nudged his gun loose in its leather. He had been easy to arrest three years ago, so confident of release that he'd made no objection when Bishop came after him. But it would be different now, and Sid would soon know it.

Main Street hadn't changed at all. The reek of Joe Blair's livery stable merged with the smoky odor of Dutch Elmendorf's blacksmith shop; the business section's false-fronted buildings had the same warped wood awnings and slack-hipped stoops and tilted railings. The Spur Saloon, Seligman's Mercantile, and the Acme Hotel were all the same; the ancient clock in the belfry atop the courthouse still showed the incorrect time of 10:33, as it had for a decade. But because he was not as he had been three years ago, the town didn't *feel* the same to Jim Maiben.

He was thinking about that when he turned in at the livery stable where Joe Blair sat in the shadowed runway.

"So you came back," the fat liveryman greeted, hoisting his huge bulk off the bench.

But Blair didn't offer to shake hands, and Maiben thought, He still thinks I burned that shack.

It was the same at the saloon. Bald Mike Finnigan was civil enough as he served a drink, but that was all. Maiben remembered that Mike had served on the jury, as had Joe Blair and Abe Seligman. All twelve of those men had been Tonto Bend citizens and they'd all thought him guilty.

Thinking back to the trial, Maiben recalled the circuit judge's scathing charge to the jury: "Arson is a despicable crime — a furtive, premeditated crime accomplished by stealth. A crime against which there is no defense — no way a man can protect his home or place of business."

And the jury had peered at him as if seeing something lower than snake sign in a wheel rut. . . .

Maiben toyed with his glass of bourbon, feeling no need for hurry. "Town seems real quiet," he offered tentatively.

Finnigan nodded. "Settlers busy with their crops. Cowmen all broke."

"Is Sid Bishop in town?" Maiben asked.

"Him and Bart Volpert had a drink here half an hour ago."

"I didn't think Bart drank whisky," Maiben said.

"He don't. Bart took sody pop."

Ernie Wade came from the rear of the saloon where the card room was. He said disgustedly, "Damnedest luck a man ever had. Got beat with three tens."

His bloodshot eyes held the dazed expression of a man half-drunk, and he didn't seem to recognize Maiben until he bellied up to the bar. Then surprise altered his eyes and some swift antagonism deepened the frown ruts on his heavy, dissipated face. "So you're back!" he muttered, as if in accusation.

"Any objections?" Maiben asked mildly.

The question seemed to baffle Wade. He rubbed the bristle of whiskers on his chin for a moment before saying, "Maybe yes, and maybe no."

"Free country, ain't it?" Maiben inquired, guessing the reason for this man's animosity, and amused by it.

"Maybe it ain't so free as you think," Wade muttered, anger staining his beefy cheeks. Then a wildness came into his eyes and he shouted, "You stay away from her, Maiben! By God, you leave her alone!"

Whereupon Wade turned away from the bar and strode to the bat-wing gates in the stiff way of a drunk forcing himself to walk straight.

Maiben glanced at Finnigan and asked amusedly, "What's eating on Ernie?"

The barkeep shrugged. "Too much booze,

or too much woman. Might be some of both."

It was, Maiben thought, a sagacious opinion. Unable to satisfy Dulcie's craving for fancy clothes, Wade had probably tried to bolster his sagging self-respect with booze and lost Dulcie in the bargain. But Ernie still wanted her. . . .

Maiben downed his drink and walked toward the courtroom, in search of Bishop. If Hatabelle had preferred charges he wanted to know it, and wanted Bishop to understand how things stood. He was abreast of Seligman's Mercantile when Bart Volpert came from the doorway and registered his surprise by exclaiming, "Why, Jim — I didn't know you had come back!"

The same nervous, high-pitched voice, the same meek smile. Looking at Volpert now, Maiben remembered what Gail had said about mistaking him for Volpert and couldn't comprehend it. Spade's owner was tall and dark, but the resemblance ended there, for his eyes were a muddy brown and his spongy, round-cheeked face was pitted with pock marks.

"Too bad about your place being sold to Steffan," Volpert said.

Maiben shrugged, watching Volpert's eyes and seeing in them all the gutless caution that had been there three years ago; all the weakness of a man afraid to fight. He said casually, "I hear you tried to buy it."

"Well, yes, after it had been sold to Steffan," Volpert admitted, revealing his embarrassment with a sheepish smile. "I wouldn't have tried to buy it otherwise, Jim. Not a friend's place."

"Were we friends?" Maiben inquired bluntly.

That startled Volpert. His brown eyes narrowed, and for this brief moment he searched Maiben's face as if seeking the answer to some momentous question — as if demanding it. Then the sheepish smile returned, and he said, "Well, we were neighbors and never had no trouble."

Maiben nodded agreement to that, thinking that the same could be said for every other rancher in the hills. Bart Volpert never had trouble with anyone — not real trouble. He was too goddamn spineless. "What caused George Jessop's death?" Maiben asked.

"Heart attack. He had organized a building bee for a family in Burro Alley whose house burned down. He closed up his bank that day and worked right along with the rest of them, until the house was finished by lantern light that evening. Then he went home and was eating supper when his heart let go. He was too old to work like that, I guess. Sure had a big funeral. Seemed like everybody in Rampage Basin attended it."

"Should think they would, considering that George had done 'em all favors," Maiben muttered. "He never met a stranger or quit a friend in need."

As Maiben turned away, Volpert asked, "Have you heard about me being married?"

"Yeah. Never thought you were that romantic."

Volpert's chuckle was almost a giggle. "Surprised myself," he said, and walked on.

Maiben stood there for a moment, idly watching Volpert cross to where his horse stood at the Spur hitchrack. The animal, a solid bay with black points, reminded Maiben of the horse he'd bought in Yuma. That was one thing he and Bart had in common: a liking for solid-colored horses. When Volpert rode away from the hitchrack Maiben observed that there was a gun scabbard strapped to the saddle, but it was empty. Spade's owner, he reflected, might carry a rifle on occasion to shoot varmints while riding the range, but that was about all. So thinking, Maiben sauntered on to the courthouse.

Sheriff Sid Bishop sat tilted back with

both boots propped on his desk, a medium-sized man whose age-sagged face brightened with a benevolent smile as Maiben came into the office. "Welcome home," he greeted, and shook hands.

He was, Maiben thought, a born politician. Sid had a knack for being friends with everyone. Cowman, settler, the well-to-do on Residential Avenue, or the poor in Burro Alley; it made no difference to Sid. Bishop wore a friendly smile in the same habitual way he wore a star pinned to his vest. It was part of his job. . . .

"Has Clyde Hatabelle been in to see you today?" Maiben inquired.

Bishop shook his head and asked, "Some reason why you thought he would?"

Ignoring that question, Maiben told Bishop about the shooting at Spanish Spring, and afterward, at Roman Six. "Somebody wants my scalp," he said.

"Now who would do a thing like that?" Bishop demanded in frowning puzzlement. "It makes no more sense than Steffan being shot at, or the calf-stealing. I've been at my wit's end, trying to figure it out."

He looked, Maiben thought, like a thoroughly worried sheriff; like a man beset by more trouble than he knew how to handle. . . .

"Bart Volpert came to see me an hour ago," Bishop said. "His calf crop is being run off four and five at a time. Every ranch in the Barricades will go broke if it keeps up."

"Do you think Clyde Hatabelle is behind it?" Maiben asked.

Bishop gawked at him as if doubting his sanity. "What a damn fool question!" he exclaimed. "Clyde is a land agent, not a cow thief."

Maiben shrugged. "Somebody is behind it. Somebody who's smart enough to run a real smooth deal."

It occurred to Maiben now that the man who had shot at him might not be involved with the rustling at all, or with Steffan's shooting. He asked, "Did you get a notice from Yuma that I was going to be released on a certain date?"

"Yes," Bishop said. "That's routine procedure."

"Did you tell anyone?"

Bishop scratched his head. "Suppose I mentioned it, which would be natural. But can't recollect just who to."

"Ernie Wade?"

"Well, I might've. Why?"

Maiben said thoughtfully, "He seems to have a grudge against me," and wondered if

Wade had shot at him last night. That might explain why the dry gulcher had run off so quickly after each attack.

"You think it might've been Ernie?" Bishop inquired.

Maiben shrugged. "No way of telling, but I intend to find out."

"Me, too," Bishop assured. "I'll keep an eye on Ernie. He's gone all haywire since his wife quit him. Acts loco in the head."

Presently, as Maiben was leaving the office, he turned in the doorway and said, "One thing more, Sid. Jails don't agree with me. I won't be arrested again without a fight."

"How you mean that?" Bishop demanded.

"Just like it sounds," Maiben said, and went out to the street.

Deciding that he needed a haircut, a shave, and a bath, he went into Sam Meaker's barbershop. Meaker was reading a copy of the Tombstone Epitaph. He looked up as Maiben entered, and letting the paper fall from his hands, sat as if paralyzed by some overwhelming astonishment or apprehension.

Maiben peered at him in scowling puzzlement. He asked, "Why you gawking at me like that?"

The pale-faced barber didn't seem to hear

him. Meaker said nervously, "I only did my duty, like the rest of them."

"The rest of who?"

"The jury."

And while Maiben continued his questing appraisal, Meaker said urgently, "I'm a married man with three small children to support. You wouldn't shoot a man with a wife and three kids, would you?"

Maiben understood it then, and felt like laughing. This fluttery-fingered barber had served on the jury which had convicted him. Now Meaker feared an ex-convict's reprisal. Masking his amusement, Maiben asked gravely, "Three kids? I thought it was only one."

"No, it's three. My wife has had two babies since you left."

"Boys or girls?"

"The two new ones were both girls," Meaker said earnestly. "They've got blue eyes, like their mother. Beautiful babies."

"Blue-eyed girls," Maiben said, as if considering that fact important. Who, he wondered, had convinced this gutless barber his life was in danger because an ex-convict had returned?

"A widow with three small children would be a sad thing," Meaker suggested.

"Suppose so," Maiben agreed solemnly.

Hanging up his hat, he said, "I'll think it over while you give me a shave and a shearing."

Afterward, soaking in one of Meaker's tin tubs, Maiben considered what the barber had told him and understood that other men in this town felt a kindred apprehension. According to Meaker, every man who'd served on the jury feared his return. Joe Blair, the barber said, had began packing a derringer a week ago, and Mike Finnigan kept a loaded six-shooter handy at his bar. Even Dutch Elmendorf, who could smash down any man in Rampage Basin with his huge fists, had brought a Winchester to his blacksmith shop.

But the most surprising part of it was the fact that Sid Bishop had spread the news. According to Meaker, Sid had received word from Warden Stone that Jim Maiben was coming back to avenge his conviction. Yet Bishop hadn't seemed the least bit apprehensive. In fact he'd been wholly relaxed and friendly. . . .

If Sid suspected there was to be reprisal against citizens of Tonto Bend, why hadn't he shown it?

Reviewing his visit at the sheriff's office, Maiben wasn't sure whether or not Sid had had an opportunity to make a surprise draw

96

against him. That, he thought, would be the normal thing for a lawman to do: disarm a suspected troublemaker and refuse him the privilege of carrying a gun in town. But Bishop had shown no sign of nervousness or tension, which seemed odd. Even though the man hadn't had what Maiben considered a sufficient opportunity to draw his gun, there should have been some indication of tension in him.

Maiben was wondering about that as he left the barbershop. This country was full of puzzles. Life had seemed simple and reasonable here three years ago; now everything was complicated. It was ironic that men like Joe Blair and Mike Finnigan should go armed against a man who was being shot at by an unknown dry gulcher. Recalling Sam Meaker's gushy relief at being told he wouldn't be shot, Maiben grinned.

He was passing the Tonto Bend Bank when Effie Jessop beckoned to him from the doorway. Surprised at this gesture from a woman who had never seemed to approve of him, Maiben stepped to the doorway. "I'm sorry about George," he said. "He was a fine man."

Effie Jessop showed him an unsmiling face that retained more youthfulness than he remembered. She said, "George was too big-hearted for his own good. He let folks take advantage of him."

"Suppose so," Maiben agreed.

"George told me about his promise to you, but I sold your ranch because the bank was overloaded with past due mortgages. It was awful, the way George let things go. Especially with cowmen. I don't think George ever foreclosed on a cowman in his life. He seemed to think they should be given special privileges."

Maiben nodded, remembering now that she was several years younger than her husband, and lacked his conviction that cow folks were the backbone of the country.

"Just before he died, George asked me to tell you something," she reported. "Something he seemed to think was very important."

She ceased speaking and glanced past him. Some pleasant thought altered the gravity of her face; it shaped her lips to gentle smiling as she asked, "Why, Clyde — what happened to your face?"

Maiben turned, meeting Hatabelle's shifting glance and seeing the discoloration that ran from a bruised nostril to his swollen right eye. Hatabelle bowed, lifting his hat to Effie Jessop and giving her a gallant smile. "An accident in the dark last night," he said, and walked on, ignoring Maiben's presence.

A queer mixture of amusement and anger rose in Jim Maiben. The land agent was running true to form, making no remark that might bring on a fight. But the sight of him made Maiben itch to finish the job he'd begun last night at Roman Six. At this moment he regretted his promise to Gail Steffan, and felt like a witless fool for having made it.

Effie Jessop watched Hatabelle until he turned in at the post office. Her eyes held more pleasure and more warmth than Maiben had ever seen in them; she seemed to vibrate with suppressed emotion, and Maiben thought, She's got a case on Hatabelle. Everyone, it seemed, liked the land agent, one way or another. Everyone except Jim Maiben. . . .

He asked, "What did George say to tell me?"

Effie's smile faded. She glanced over her shoulder as if to make sure no one else was within sound of her voice. "It doesn't make sense to me, but George said for you to watch Sid Bishop."

"Watch Sid Bishop?" Maiben echoed. "Why?"

"George didn't say. He was dying at the time, poor man. He tried to tell me something else. But he just didn't have the breath."

A customer came to the doorway then, and she said, "Excuse me, please."

"Well, thanks," Maiben said, so baffled that he could scarcely think straight. Walking over to the hotel veranda and taking a chair, he put his mind to the task of solving the riddle of Jessop's warning.

What had George known, or suspected, about Sheriff Bishop?

There must be some connection between the burning of Ike Fenton's shack and the message Effie had given him, Maiben reasoned; yet he could think of none. All Sid had done was arrest a man accused of arson. If Jessop's warning had named Clyde Hatabelle, or Ernie Wade, or even Red Pomeroy, it would have made some sense. But George had named Bishop.

Maiben shaped up a cigarette and idly watched Alamo Rand drive away from the livery-stable corral with his family. There, he reflected soberly, was another victim of the mysterious trouble that was disrupting this once peaceful country. It seemed monstrous that an industrious family man should have to give up his home because some sneaky fanatic stole weanling calves and shot at men from ambush. Remembering that Helen Rand had mistaken him for Volpert, Maiben thought, Perhaps we do look alike, from a distance.

That reminded him of his feeling about Volpert's marriage — how it had seemed important in some remote way. There appeared to be no connection between that and Jessop's warning, yet he couldn't discard the vague notion that each had something to do with what was happening in the Barricade Hills.

Maiben saw Hatabelle come out of the post office and walk east along Main Street. Would the land agent ask Bishop to arrest him on a charge of assault? Not likely, Maiben thought, and now, as Dulcie Todd came from the Bon Ton Millinery, he watched her with growing interest as she crossed Main Street's wide dust.

Ernie Wade needed a drink. He had intended to ask Mike Finnigan for one on credit, but sight of Jim Maiben at the bar had spoiled that. Being broke was disgrace enough, without having to admit it in front of Dulcie's old sweetheart. Ernie cursed, recalling his wife's bragging talk about Maiben. You'd think, by God, that he was the greatest man who ever lived, instead of being a jailbird. Jim was so romantic; Jim

101

was this, and Jim was that.

To hear her tell it he'd been the perfect lover, until the law grabbed him. . . .

All during their marriage it had galled Ernie that his wife had been Maiben's girl. The knowledge of that intimacy scorched his soul; it spawned jealous resentment toward the man who'd had her first. And Dulcie, damn her, had seemed to enjoy teasing him with the fact — tantalizing him by recalling incidents of Maiben's courtship. Once, when he'd threatened to hit her if she mentioned Maiben again, Dulcie had laughed at him and asked, "What difference does it make? I'm in bed with you, aren't I?"

And now Jim Maiben was back. To Ernie's way of thinking there was only one reason for his return. Maiben's ranch was gone, and there were no big outfits in Rampage Basin where a man could get a job punching cows. What other reason was there, except to renew his old affair with Dulcie?

"Damn him to hell!" Ernie muttered.

Turning into Burro Alley, he tried to remember if there was a drink left in the bottle at his shack. When a mongrel puppy sniffed at his leg in friendly fashion, Ernie kicked it, and then cursed the Mexican boy who rushed out to retrieve the yelping dog.

An old woman sitting in a hovel's blanket-draped doorway scolded Ernie in Spanish. When he swore at her she spat through toothless gums and shrilled, "Borrachin!"

This, Ernie thought, was a hell of a place for him to be living — on the cheapest, dirtiest street in Tonto Bend. And it wasn't even a street, just an alley. Again as he had a thousand times, Ernie cursed himself for having sold his ranch. Town life had seemed good at first. Living with Dulcie in a stylish cottage on Residential Avenue, he'd been happy as a lark. She had been his sweet-loving wife, with a body that made a man itch just to look at it. Thinking back to those nights on Residential Avenue and comparing it with what he had now, Ernie cursed morosely.

It didn't seem possible that there could be so much change in so short a time. A few short months ago he had been a man with a wife — the prettiest wife in town. And he'd been proud as a peacock, knowing that other men envied him. Seeing how they looked at Dulcie he'd thought, Don't you wish you had her? and felt greater than Billy-be-damn.

But not now. Everything was wrong, and

it all went back to Jim Maiben, who'd had Dulcie first. . . .

CHAPTER SEVEN

Dulcie Todd came up the hotel veranda steps and exclaimed, "Jim — you've come back!" in a smiling, thoroughly pleased way.

She wore a little straw hat trimmed with black lace that formed a coquettish fringe over her eyes and matched the ruffle on her stylish white blouse. Accepting the hand she offered, Maiben remembered that Dulcie had always been dressy — that she'd once told him most of her wages went for clothes.

"So you're a married woman," Maiben said, strongly aware of her lilac perfume and the intimate pressure of her fingers.

Dulcie shook her head. "Not any more," she said, the smile fading from her heart-shaped face. "It was all a mistake, Jim. A horrible mistake."

Her pouty lips were as Maiben remembered them: *kissing* lips, he reflected. And her dark eyes, so warmly shining, reminded him of past pleasures. She had never been much inclined to conceal her feelings; at this moment she wanted to attract male attention and showed it in the frankly receptive way she smiled at him. "You haven't changed at all," she said. "You're just as handsome as ever." Then, appraising his soiled and threadbare riding pants, she said, "You need some new clothes."

"That's not all I need," Maiben said, thinking of the few dollars he possessed.

But Dulcie accepted a different meaning; she laughed at him and said teasingly, "The same old Jim."

A born flirt, Maiben thought, and wondered why he hadn't realized it three years ago. Everything about her — the lace-trimmed hat, the frank teasing of her eyes, the peekaboo blouse, and perfume — was man bait. Yet even now, knowing what she was and recalling how casually she had discarded a prison-bound sweetheart, some portion of the old attraction remained. Less impelling, perhaps, and distilled of ingredients that brewed a cheaper wine. But it held a basic and tantalizing flavor for a man who'd been long gone from women. . . .

"The same Dulcie," Maiben mused, and added tauntingly, "the only girl who ever gave me back a ring."

That mildly spoken accusation banished

the pleasure from her eyes. "Oh, Jim — can't you forget that?" she asked urgently. "Can't you understand how upset and half-crazy I was? Your going to prison for three years seemed like the end of the world to me."

"Well, it didn't seem exactly inviting to me either," Maiben said cynically. "But you didn't think about my part of it."

She reached out and grasped his sleeve; she said, "I know, Jim. It was awful of me. But I was so surprised and disappointed. After all the plans we'd made it was like being kicked in the face, as if nothing was worth planning for, or waiting for. It upset me terribly."

"Is that why you married Ernie Wade?" Maiben inquired dryly.

Dulcie shook her head. "I don't know what possessed me, Jim. Guess I was all at loose ends after you left. I couldn't get over the fact you'd told me to go to hell."

"What else did you expect me to say?"

"Well, you didn't need to say that. I know it wasn't very nice of me to give back the ring like I did. But women do queer things when they're upset, Jim. Foolish things they're sorry for afterward. You're old enough to know that."

Maiben grinned, thinking of what had

happened at Spanish Spring when he took Gail Steffan in his arms. He said, "I'm old enough to understand women, but not smart enough."

"You always seemed to understand me all right," Dulcie reminded him with mock censure. "You knew how to get around me any time you wanted some loving." She sighed, as if regretting a past that she was half ashamed of; she said softly, "We had good times together, didn't we, Jim?"

Maiben nodded, and seeing the promise of more good times frankly revealed in her eyes, said grinningly, "We did, for a fact."

She turned to the doorway now and peered in at the lobby clock. She said, "I must go to work now, but I'll be through at nine."

Then, seeing Ernie Wade step up behind Maiben, she screamed.

Maiben whirled and threw up a protecting arm. But it was too late. Wade's fist hit him in the face with an impact that knocked him sideways. Maiben was attempting to regain his balance when he tripped over a chair; Ernie caught him flush on the chin with a hard right that knocked him down.

Sprawled on the veranda's dusty boards, Maiben was remotely aware of being booted in the ribs, and hearing Dulcie's cry: "Ernie

— don't!"

As Maiben struggled to his knees, Wade leaned over and aimed a looping right at his face. Maiben ducked so that Ernie's knuckles barely grazed his jaw; he was getting up when Ernie kicked at him again. Maiben grabbed the boot and rose with it, tipping Wade over. Ernie landed on his back, and for the moment it took him to regain his feet, Maiben stood there dazedly shaking his head and hearing excited voices in the street.

"I'll learn you to fuss with my wife!" Wade yelled and lunged at Maiben with both fists swinging.

Maiben backed up. He took successive blows on his guarding arms and shoulders. He kept his chin tucked against his chest.

"Fight, you smart-alecky son!" Ernie raged. "Stand and fight!"

But Maiben, needing time for his head to clear, kept circling and backing. As if from a distance he heard Dulcie demand, "Why don't you stop it, Sheriff Sid?"

A crowd had gathered now, and more people were coming, attracted by the meaty smack of fists on flesh. Sam Meaker, who had come from his barbershop with a lathered brush in his hand, asked worriedly, "Ain't he liable to use his gun?"

"He'd better not," Joe Blair announced, revealing the derringer in his hand. "Ernie is unarmed."

For a little interval, while Maiben collided with another chair and floundered against the veranda railing in desperate retreat, he had only a distorted impression of his attacker. There was a dull throbbing in his temples and now he became aware of aching ribs. He blinked his eyes, trying to dispell the sleazy fog that dimmed them; he heard Dulcie's urgent voice announcing, "Jim isn't able to fight, Sid. He's hurt, and you should stop it!"

Maiben backed into the hotel's front wall and bounced off it, going into a desperate clinch. Wade clawed Maiben's clutching arms; he cursed and tugged and twisted, using elbows and knees before he finally pulled free. "I'll learn you," he panted, swinging at Maiben's face. "I'll learn you good!"

But the hard-won respite had given Maiben's head time to clear and now, as his eyes came into focus, he glimpsed Wade's scowling face above a pair of punching fists. Wheeling sharply and drawing Wade off balance, Maiben swung his first blow, catching Ernie in the chest. He said rankly, "Now we fight," and taking a left on an unhunched shoulder, targeted Ernie's rage-rutted face.

For a long moment of sheer brutality, Maiben stood toe to toe with Wade, striking and being struck, until he broke that up with what looked like another retreat. But as Wade pitched forward in eager pursuit, Maiben tripped him. Evading Ernie's clutching hands, he stood with both fists cocked while Wade fell on his face.

A yeasty sigh rose from the crowd. A man yelled, "Git up, Ernie — git up!"

Maiben waited, sensing where the crowd's sympathy was. These gawking spectators were for Ernie; they wanted to see him lick an ex-convict. . . .

Ernie got up slowly, blood dribbling from his nostrils. He tried to evade Maiben's fists, and partially succeeded, taking the blow on an upflung arm. But the next one caught him on the nose. Wade bellowed a curse that turned into a grunt as Maiben slammed him in the belly. When Ernie's hands came down instinctively, Maiben slashed with a left that clouted Wade's bleeding nose again. He heard Wade groan, and saw the bloody smear his fist made against Ernie's cheek; he rolled with an ineffectual blow that barely grazed his jaw, and then slugged Wade in the belly just below his high-arched ribs.

Ernie loosed a wooshing gasp. He was bending forward, clutching his hurt belly with both hands, when Maiben caught him under the chin with a vicious uppercut.

Wade went over backwards, crashing against the cap-sized chair. He sat motionless for a moment, a silly, lop-sided smile on his battered face, both hands limply resting on the veranda floor. Then, as if observing the blood that dribbled onto his sweat-sogged shirt, Wade lifted an arm and wiped his nose on a shirt sleeve.

Maiben watched Sid Bishop climb over the veranda, railing, and for the first time identified faces in the crowd on the sidewalk. Joe Blair, great paunched and sharp-eyed, stood beside Dutch Elmendorf whose soot-smeared face revealed an avid interest in these proceedings; Clyde Hatabelle, Abe Seligman, Mike Finnigan — everyone in town seemed to be in the crowd of gawking spectators.

The impact of all those watchful eyes reminded Maiben of the day he'd stood in the courtroom for sentencing. It gave him the same morose feeling of aloneness; of being rejected by the pack. They had been against him then. They were against him now.

"What," Sid Bishop inquired, "was this all about?"

Maiben shrugged.

But Dulcie said, loud enough for all to hear, "About me, I guess." She smiled, and gave Maiben a brief, pleased glance. "Jim and I were talking about old times when Ernie came up and hit him."

Bishop bent over Wade and helped him to his feet. "You'd better come over to the jail and sober up," he suggested.

Ernie shook his head. "I ain't drunk," he muttered, wiping his nose again.

"Well, come over and wash up, then," Bishop said, taking him by the arm.

Dulcie came over to Maiben. She touched his bruised jaw with exploring fingers and asked solicitously, "Does it hurt?"

Embarrassed by the crowd's watching eyes, Maiben shook his head. This, he supposed, would make an interesting story for the town's gossips; it would be discussed in every home on Residential Avenue.

"I've got to go in now," Dulcie said. "See you at suppertime, Jim."

Still feeling conspicuous, but refusing to reveal it, Maiben walked over to a chair and sat down. Ignoring the crowd which was now breaking up, he gave his attention to fashioning a cigarette. To hell with them, he

113

thought, and guessing that Dulcie had taken a perverse pleasure in having two men fight over her, resented her too. It occurred to him that for some odd reason he felt no animosity toward Wade. The man was loco with jealousy and regret. Guessing how it had been with him these past few months, Maiben felt sorry for Ernie. He had lost his ranch and the woman who talked him into selling it. Ernie, he guessed, was what Mike Finnigan had said he was — a victim of too much booze and too much woman. That combination had ruined countless men. . . .

Sheriff Bishop stood at the open gate of a cell and watched Wade wash his face. "Your nose'll be big as a balloon tomorrow," he said amusedly. "You took somewhat of a licking."

"The smart alecky bastard will pay for it," Ernie promised in an outraged voice. "He'll pay plenty, by God. I'll fix him so's he won't honeyfuss with my wife — or anybody else's."

"How?" Bishop inquired.

Ernie wiped his fist-marked face. He said sullenly, "I'll fix him."

"Not with your fists," Bishop disagreed. "Remember how Maiben flattened Ike Fenton on the Spur stoop. Ike outweighed

Jim by twenty pounds, but when that fight was finished you'd think Ike had been tromped by six shod broncs. Jim is a rank man with his fists. Tol'able rank."

Ernie peered at the sheriff, a thoughtful expression coming into his bloodshot eyes. "Well, there's other ways," he muttered. Contemplating Sid's friendly smile, he added, "I've got a gun at the shack."

The smile faded from Bishop's face. He said, "That might get you into trouble, Ernie. I don't blame a man for being touchy about his ex-wife. There's always a chance of getting her back, if you can keep the romeos away from her. But some folks might not feel the same way about it. Especially if Maiben was shot right here in town. People are funny that way, Ernie. They'll overlook all sorts of things, like a man fooling with another man's wife or beating the hell out of somebody. But not murder. And that's what it would be, if you shot Maiben here in town."

"What you mean by that?" Wade demanded.

Bishop shrugged.

"You mean it should be done up in the hills?" Ernie asked.

"Well, I'm not saying it should be done at all," Bishop explained patiently. Accompanying Wade out to the office, he cautioned, "Maiben might be real quick with a gun. By the look of that holster he's wearing he might've done some practicing lately. I'd think twice, was I you, about starting any shootout on the street with him."

Then, as Clyde Hatabelle came up to the office doorway, Bishop motioned for Wade to go on outside.

"What happened to your face?" Bishop inquired.

Hatabelle said ruefully, "An accident in the dark."

He watched until Wade reached the sidewalk, then announced, "There was trouble at North Fork again last night. A man on horseback ripped out the control gate sometime after midnight. Three fields were flooded before the break was discovered — washed out completely. In addition to the crop damage, the waste of all that water is tragic, Sid. It means we won't have enough to last through the summer."

Bishop nodded sympathetically. He asked, "Was the rider seen?"

"No, but his horse tracks were plain enough. Four settlers followed him into the hills for nearly ten miles today, then lost the trail on those rocky benches below West Divide."

116

"You figure it was a cowman?"

When Hatabelle nodded, the sheriff asked, "Which one?"

Hatabelle shrugged, his bruised face wholly grave. "I want to be fair, Sid. I'm admitting this isn't the first time we've had night rider trouble at North Fork. But I happen to know that Jim Maiben was back before sundown yesterday — and that he hates me."

"So?" Bishop mused. "Well, it's a thought. Jim always was against those settlers."

Hatabelle nodded. "He has lost his ranch, and is as bitter as a man could be. Seems to have only one thing left — an insane desire for revenge."

Bishop peered at Hatabelle's discolored face. He asked slyly, "Is Maiben the accident you met up with?"

"Well, yes. At Roman Six. I stopped by there to offer Eric Steffan help with his haying, and Maiben jumped me. But I don't blame him much, Sid. It was my testimony that convicted him. I still think he was the man I saw the day Fenton's shack was burned. But there's a bare chance I might've been mistaken."

Bishop shook his head. "Now, Clyde, that's no way for you to talk," he counseled. Opening a desk drawer he took out a revolver and handed it to Hatabelle. "You carry this, and use it, if Maiben tackles you again."

Hatabelle accepted the gun, and peered at it as if repelled by the thought of its destructiveness. "Don't believe I could shoot a man," he admitted solemnly.

"In self-defense, you could," Bishop insisted. He gave the land agent a benevolent smile, adding, "Self-preservation is the first law of nature, Clyde. You'd better start remembering that."

"Perhaps," Hatabelle admitted. He walked to the doorway, and stopping there, said thoughtfully, "I'd like to talk to Maiben. I'd like to have him understand why I had to do what I did. There was nothing personal about it. Just something I had to do, as a citizen with certain obligations to tell the truth."

"You'd be wasting your time," Bishop scoffed. "Maiben is what he is — and talk won't change him none at all."

CHAPTER EIGHT

Burro Smith arrived in Tonto Bend at sundown, riding a line-backed grulla mule and leading a burro loaded with firewood. A tall, round-shouldered scarecrow in a tattered cotton shirt and bachelor-patched pants, he rode in the loosely slumped fashion of a drunken man. But Smith was stark sober. Beneath the floppy brim of an ancient sombrero his milk-blue eyes held the unblemished clarity of a woodland lake, and upon his leathery beard-bristled face was the wistful eagerness of a man motivated by high purpose.

There were people in Tonto Bend who considered Burro Smith a disgrace to mankind, especially the respectable ladies who lived on Residential Avenue. "A shiftless, prideless bum," they called him and deplored the laxity of a social order which made existence possible for such renegades. Their husbands also spoke derisively of

Smith, making jokes about his wild dream of discovering a bonanza in the Sierra Madres. "A witless rainbow chaser," they said. But each spring, when Smith headed out with his burros to spend the summer prospecting, these same men looked upon him with secret envy. . . .

Turning into the wagon yard east of Seligman's Mercantile, Smith dismounted and walked around to the rear door. His moccasined feet made no sound as he entered and stood at the rear of the store, waiting for Abe Seligman who was talking to Joe Blair.

"I don't think he intends to cause us any trouble, and neither does Sheriff Sid," the merchant said.

Blair shrugged. "Maybe not. But I'm packing this derringer until I'm certain sure."

As the liveryman turned toward the front doorway, Seligman asked, "Did Maiben mention how long he was staying in town?"

Blair shook his head and went on out to the street, whereupon Burro Smith asked, "Is Jim Maiben back from jail?"

"Yes, and in trouble already."

"What'd he do now?"

"Pounded Ernie Wade insensible on the Acme Veranda."

Burro grinned. "Jim always was a scrapper," he mused. "I'm pure tickled that he's back."

"Well, you're the only one who is," Seligman said sourly. "How many loads did you bring?"

"Just one," Burro admitted a trifle sheepishly. "It's too hot for wood choppin' these days. A man might founder hisself if he ain't careful."

Seligman made a derisive, slapping gesture with his right hand. Going out to look at the wood, he said, "The day you founder yourself working I'll believe in miracles — or Sierra Madre gold."

Afterward, when Seligman had paid him, Smith hurried over to the Spur Saloon, confident that his old friend would be there. Finding the bar deserted, he asked, "Ain't Jim Maiben in town?"

Finnigan nodded.

"Then why ain't he here?"

"Probably eating supper at the hotel," Finnigan suggested.

"Supper? What would a man want with supper his first day back from jail?"

Finnigan shrugged. "Some folks are funny that way. Come supper time they eat, regardless."

"Well, give me bourbon," Smith ordered. "Then I'll go fetch Jim for a real celebration. It must've been bad for him cooped up in jail with no whisky." He thought about that for a moment before adding slyly, "And no wimmin. Jim had a weakness for the sweet stuff. He should've been with me on the Mesa Elcampanero last summer. Some of them Mayo squaws are prettier'n a red-wheeled wagon."

Finnigan held the bottle and glass, poised for pouring. He asked, "You got some money?"

Smith gawked at him, as if baffled by such inquisitiveness. "What makes you ask such a foolish question?"

Finnigan waited, neither explaining or tilting the bottle until Burro placed a silver dollar on the bar. Then he poured the drink and placing it before Smith, snared the silver dollar without delay.

"Anybody'd think my word was no good," Burro complained.

Finnigan bounced the coin on the bar and listened to its ring. He said, "This is good," and made change.

Jim Maiben ate supper in the hotel dining room with Dulcie giving him special attention. "Seems like old times," she said, spending all her idle time at his table. "Almost like you'd never been away."

It didn't seem so to Maiben. He felt as if he were a stranger here; aware of the contemplative glances of other diners he felt conspicuous and ill at ease. He knew most of them by name, but they averted their eyes and passed his table without speaking. He thought resentfully, So this is how they treat an ex-convict. You'd think he had been convicted of murder instead of arson.

Clyde Hatabelle came into the dining room with Effie Jessop. Watching him escort her to a table, Maiben wondered at this seeming disloyalty to Gail Steffan. Was Hatabelle two-timing Gail, or merely playing up to Effie for business reasons? It didn't seem logical that a man would risk losing a girl like Gail. Perhaps the land agent needed a bank loan, or the renewal of a mortgage and was being nice to George's widow for that purpose.

Recalling the message Effie had given him, Maiben wondered if she had divulged it to Hatabelle. Probably not, for she'd acted quite secretive about it, as if ashamed that George should have used his last breath for such nonsense. . . .

Dulcie brought him a second cup of coffee. Leaning over to place it on the table, she rested her bosom against his shoulder and whispered, "Have you rented a room for tonight?"

Guessing what was in her mind, Maiben said solemnly, "Well, I thought maybe I'd bunk down in an empty still at Blair's barn."

"Oh, Jim — you're funning," Dulcie accused, and went back to the kitchen.

When Maiben finished his meal and walked through the lobby he saw Dulcie leaving the desk and understood that she had seen his name on the register. She sure seemed anxious to make up for what she'd done three years ago. You'd think he still owned a ranch, the way she played up to him. Or had a hell-smear of money in his pocket. Maiben chuckled, thinking that the joke would be on her this time. He would have his fun while the forty dollars lasted, then say good-by. And if she made any fuss he'd tell her to go to hell again.

Sauntering out to the veranda bench, Maiben sat there enjoying the first cigar he had smoked since leaving Tonto Bend. This, he reflected, was a bit different than it had been at Yuma. He was shaved, sheared and bathed, had eaten in style and been served by a waitress with romantic notions. He thought amusedly, I'm living high off the hog.

But he wouldn't be for long, not on forty dollars. The time wasn't far off when he would have to secure a riding job on one of the big outfits in Sulphur Springs Valley, or over on the San Pedro. Maiben grimaced, disliking the thought of starting all over again. A man would have to save and scrimp for upwards of ten years to get a stake; it had taken him that long, working for wages, to get his start at Roman Six.

He wondered if Gail Steffan had waited supper for him at the ranch, and hoped she hadn't. It might be a day or two before he showed up there again; perhaps longer. Even though he couldn't understand George Jessop's warning, it was the one thing he had to go by; the only definite clue that might somehow reveal the man who had burned Ike Fenton's shack. It would take some waiting, most likely, but he had done plenty of that.

It was coming dusk when Clyde Hatabelle came out and said urgently, "I'd like to talk things over, Jim."

Masking his astonishment, Maiben asked, "What things?"

"Well, about me testifying in court. That wasn't a personal matter at all. I was convinced it was you I saw that day. If it wasn't, I'm — well, there's no way of saying how sorry I am."

Maiben peered at him for a moment

before saying, "You couldn't be as sorry as me. You didn't lose three years of your life, and a ranch to boot."

The land agent shook his head, visibly distressed. "I can't believe I was mistaken," he insisted. "But even if you were guilty I want you to understand that my testimony was not a personal thing. It was an obligation that any honest citizen would accept." Then he asked, "Are you going to help Eric Steffan get in his hay?"

"Not for the next few days," Maiben muttered. "I've got other plans."

And now, seeing Burro Smith come up the veranda steps, Maiben announced cheerfully, "Here comes one of them right now."

"Jim — you old scallywag!" Smith greeted with the delighted screech of a mountain man arriving at rendezvous. "By grab, you're a sight for this son's sore eyes!"

They shook hands in the violent, knuckle-crushing fashion of old friends after long separation and cursed each other affectionately. Ignoring Hatabelle, who stood watching this, Maiben led Smith to the bench and asked, "How's things in Mexico?"

"Fine, just fine," Burro said. "Still lots of game in the Sierra Madres. Gold there too, if a man could find it."

126

Maiben grinned at him, remembering that this bright-eyed man had spent upwards of fifteen summers searching for a bonanza that might not exist. The annual failures didn't seem to dent Burro's optimism at all. Few men in Tonto Bend could match his good humor and his zest for living. The thought came to Maiben now that finding the gold might not be the important thing to Burro; perhaps it was the searching that kept him happy. . . .

"I got way over into the Yaqui country last summer," Smith reported. "Now there's a place to make your eyes bug big as slop buckets. I mean it's rougher'n the hair on a grizzly bear's belly. Rough and wild. Not a bob-wire fence in the whole shebang. There's a bunch of Mayos livin' on top of a high mesa called Elcampanero. They're the damnedest breed of Injuns you ever saw. Been livin' up there for years and got so inbred they're all shirt-tail relations to each other. They raise wheat, corn, chili and the prettiest female wimmin you ever saw. Lots of them are blondes with blue eyes and shaped like a sheepherder's dream."

"Sounds like a good place to spend the summer," Maiben suggested.

"The best ever," Burro agreed. "If they take a shine to you a feller couldn't be amongst better friends. And a white man can just about have his pick of the gals. An old chief will go through some rigmarole and then you are a Mayo Injun with a blue-eyed blanket squaw."

Hatabelle and Effie Jessop went down the veranda steps and walked toward the bank.

"Seems like we should go celebrate with some bourbon," Smith suggested.

Maiben watched Hatabelle leave Effie at the bank's outside stairway which led to the second-floor living quarters. Reminded now of the message she had given him, Maiben observed that the sheriff's office was dark. Bishop, he guessed, would be showing up for supper soon. He said, "I'm waiting for a fellow I want to see, Burro. We'll have a drink later."

Dulcie came out onto the veranda. She stood by the doorway for a moment, waiting for Maiben to notice her; then she said, "Well, I'm through work, Jim."

Maiben went over and handed her the key to his room. He said, "I'll be up after a bit."

"How long?"

"Soon as I have a little visit with Burro Smith."

"Well, I like that!" Dulcie protested poutingly. "Making me wait while you visit with a dirty old bum."

128

"He's not much older than I am" Maiben muttered, "and not much dirtier."

Whereupon he walked back to Burro, wondering if Smith had heard what she said, and hoping he hadn't. Dulcie had a hell of a nerve, thinking a man would run upstairs every time a tarty female smiled at him. Especially a man who'd got along without her for three years.

"See you've still got an eye for the sweet stuff," Burro reflected. Then, as if eager to report a pleasurable experience that should be shared with a friend, he said, "Them Mayos sure feed a man. They'll kill a couple deer, some turkeys and goats and barbecue all the meat together with plenty of chili gravy and *tortillas.* Then they'll top it off with more mescal than a man can drink."

He sighed, thinking back; he said, "They treat a white man like he's a king. Don't make no difference how much coin he's got in his pocket, or what kind of clothes he's wearin'. Not like here. Just bein' a man is all that matters with them Mayos. The women, in particular. If you're a man they're satisfied, and pleasured to be your woman. This son will be goin' back there, come spring."

Presently he asked, "How long you got to wait for the jigger you're watchin' for? I'm downright thirsty."

"No telling," Maiben said. Digging out a gold-eagle he handed it to Burro and suggested, "Go buy a quart and we'll have us a drink right here in private."

"An elegant notion," Smith agreed. "You still cotton to bourbon?"

Maiben nodded and watched Burro cross Main Street. It seemed odd that Smith, who had no more home than a tumbleweed, should be the one to make him feel at home in Tonto Bend. It would have been the same with George Jessop, were he alive. Maiben shook his head, not understanding why two men who were such direct opposites should have been his only friends.

He was watching Burro return with a bottle cradled in his right arm, when Sid Bishop came through the Spur's lamplit doorway. Observing that the sheriff turned toward his house at the west end of Main Street, Maiben got up. George Jessop had used his dying breath to say: "Watch Sid Bishop."

Now Maiben thought, I'll watch him like a hawk.

Smith came up with the bottle. He pulled its cork with his teeth and said, "Take a swig for old time's sake."

Maiben took a drink and watched Burro

have his; then he said, "I've got to look for that fellow down the street." With a sly grin he added, "If I'm not back in half an hour go up to my room. It's number five."

"You got the key?" Burro asked.

"The door'll be unlocked," Maiben assured him. "Just walk right in and make yourself at home."

That suggestion pleased Burro. He said, "I ain't slept on a hotel bed in upwards of twenty years."

"Well, you'll sleep on one tonight," Maiben promised. Going down the steps he said, "If you find anybody in it tell 'em to push over."

Casually then, in the way of a man with no definite destination, Maiben walked to Residential Avenue and turned into it. Here were the homes of Tonto Bend's more prosperous citizens, their lamplit windows making cheerful blooms against the night's mealy darkness. Maiben turned west into an alley, following this trash-littered passageway past back yards and vacant lots until he came to the rear of Bishop's barn which perched closed to Sabino Arroyo. Here he waited, watching the house. The kitchen window curtain was pulled down, but the back door was open and Maiben caught the aroma of boiling coffee. Some time after that he heard an unintelligible drone of conversation, which surprised him. Bishop had been a widower living with an only daughter three years ago. Grace wouldn't be with him now, Maiben reasoned. Then to whom was Bishop talking?

CHAPTER NINE

Maiben moved to the west end of the barn, hoping for a better view of the kitchen doorway and wanting to identify Bishop's companion. A low-branched pepper-tree midway in the yard obscured his view from this new angle; going back to his former position he wondered if Burro Smith had gone up to his room. Maiben grinned, visualizing how it would be when Dulcie discovered who her visitor was. Chances were she wouldn't have the lamp lighted, in which case it might take a little time for her to find out it was Burro.

Thinking of the various possibilities, Maiben chuckled. It would serve Dulcie right if Burro got into bed with her. . . .

The kitchen light went out. Maiben heard footsteps on the back stoop and glimpsed two vague shapes moving toward the barn. Tautly listening he heard Bishop ask, "Did you saddle my horse?"

The other man said, "Yes," and presently there was a creak of saddle leather as they mounted.

Guessing that they might come out into this alley, Maiben flattened himself against the barn. He heard a gate swing on rusty hinges, and the hooftromp of walking horses, that sound rapidly diminishing.

Wholly puzzled now, Maiben felt his way past the barn. For a moment, smelling risen dust but seeing no sign of movement, he wondered what had become of the two riders. Then, as a shod hoof clanged against stone somewhere below him, Maiben understood what had happened. Bishop and his companion had ridden into Sabino Arroyo.

The significance of that discovery sent Maiben back along the dark alley. There could be but one reason why a sheriff would choose such a method of leaving town. Sid didn't want to be seen on Main Street.

Walking toward Blair's Livery, Maiben wondered what was behind Bishop's need for secrecy.

And who was his companion?

It occurred to Maiben that the sheriff had been quite gentle in his treatment of Ernie Wade. Even though Dulcie had accused Wade of starting the fight, Sid seemed reluctant to interfere. Was Ernie his companion?

If so, what were they up to?

Remembering that Clyde Hatabelle had been in town half an hour ago, Maiben understood that the land agent might be the second rider. He swore disgustedly, thinking, Hell, it might be almost anybody.

One thing, though, he was convinced of now: George Jessop's warning was founded on something more than idle conjecture. George had known something about Bishop that made him suspicious of the lawman. . . .

Maiben was cinching up his bay when Joe Blair came over from the saloon. "You leaving town so soon?" he asked.

Maiben nodded. Presently, paying for the gelding's feed, he inquired, "Did Hatabelle pull out for North Fork?"

Blair glanced at a buggy near the horse pen, and shook his head. "Leastwise Clyde's rig is still here."

But that, Maiben realized, didn't prove anything. Hatabelle could have walked to Bishop's house and waited for Sid there. Eager to find out if the two riders had headed west after crossing the arroyo, Maiben put his horse to a trot. This might lead to something; it might be the break he needed.

Crossing the bridge, Maiben turned south along the west bank of Sabino Arroyo. Lamplit windows in town made a broad pattern of illumination but here the night's quilted darkness was unbroken. Dismounting and lighting a match, he looked for horse tracks, walked on and lit another match. Finally, a quarter mile south of the bridge he found what he was looking for: a well-defined trail that came out of the arroyo with fresh hoof-prints pointing toward Apache Mesa.

Bishop, he understood then, made a practice of leaving town by this route. "Returning also," Maiben guessed and felt a rising sense of anticipation. Putting the bay into the trail he followed it westward. No telling where it would lead, or what he would find at the end of it, he reflected; but there was no doubt in his mind about Bishop now. Sid was mixed up in the rustling deal. No sheriff needed to sneak in and out of town on legitimate business.

Yet even so, Maiben could scarcely believe that Bishop would become involved in a venture that seemed so profitless. How could anyone hope to make money stealing weanling calves?

Halting occasionally to be sure that his horse was still in the trail, Maiben climbed the long steep slope to the top of Apache Mesa. There was a cool breeze here, carrying a hint of approaching autumn. Fall came early in the high country; a month from now the nights would be turning chilly in the Barricade Hills.

Maiben wondered what was happening in room number five at the Acme Hotel. Burro must've gone up there by now. Dulcie would be flabbergasted; she'd probably order Burro out of the room, when she found out who he was. Either that, or she'd grab up her clothes and hightail down the hallway to her own room. No telling what would happen; but knowing Burro, Maiben felt reasonably sure that he would spend the night in a hotel bed. Burro had been in and out of too many scrapes to let a flighty female spook him. . . .

The next time Maiben stopped to look at the ground there was no well-defined trail; merely some horse tracks, none of which were fresh. Further searching convinced him that the trail he had followed from the arroyo ended back there near the mesa's rim, with tracks fanning out from it in various directions. Finding the fresh set of hoof-prints would be a matter of luck, and more matches than he had left. So thinking, Maiben swung north to the stage road, turned into a dry wash beyond it and presently dismounted. Unsaddling, he tied the bay so that it could munch mesquite beans, then settled himself comfortably in the dry sand.

Three years ago impatience would have made this long wait for daybreak a frustrating interlude, but now Maiben accepted it with the shrugging fatalism of an Indian. That, he reflected, was one thing prison taught a man. Patience.

When Gail Steffan did the barn chores at sundown she scanned the brush-blotched flats southward, hoping to see a dust head that would signal an approaching rider. There was none, and she told herself, "I can't wait supper any longer."

Yet even then she waited until Eric Steffan predicted, "No telling when Maiben will get back. He might have circled into town and gone on a spree."

Gail had been thinking the same thing. But she said, "Oh, I don't think he would do that. Jim would've told me if he wasn't coming back for supper."

Steffan peered thoughtfully at his daughter. He asked, "Have you changed your mind about Maiben? Last night you had no liking for him at all. You said we should treat him in a friendly way so that he wouldn't take his spite out on Clyde. But now you wait supper past dark for him."

Gail shrugged and busied herself at the stove. How could she explain what she felt about Jim Maiben when she didn't understand it herself. The man was a huge puzzle of contradictions, and so were her feelings toward him. . . .

All through supper she listened for sound of Maiben's approach. She said worriedly, "He might have been shot at again. Might have been wounded, or killed, for all we know."

"So?" her father mused, smiling slyly. He nodded, as if in agreement to an unspoken question, and said, "It is not Clyde you are worried about. It is Maiben."

Gail accepted his gentle teasing without offering a defense. Afterward she said, "It must have been awful, spending all that time in prison for a thing he didn't do."

She was putting away the supper dishes an hour later when a rider came into the dark yard.

"There he is now," Steffan predicted.

Gail thought so, too. She smiled and pushed the coffee-pot to the front of the stove; she was putting a liberal helping of warmed-up potatoes into a frying pan when

Sheriff Bishop called, "Anybody home?"

Hugely disappointed, Gail went out to the stoop and peered at the lawman who sat his horse in the doorway's shaft of lamplight. "Won't you come in?" she invited.

Bishop shook his head. "Got some riding to do. How's your father?"

Steffan had hobbled to the doorway and now said, "Still useless as a spavined horse. Doc Reed says it'll be another two or three weeks before I can ride."

Gail wondered what had brought the sheriff here so late in the day. But it was characteristic of her that she didn't ask him. Instead she invited, "Won't you have a cup of coffee?"

"No, thank you, ma'am. I'm looking for the scoundrel who wrecked an irrigation gate at North Fork some time after midnight last night. Clyde Hatabelle says it was done by one rider who headed back into this country afterward. Clyde thinks it might've been Jim Maiben."

"Oh no," Gail said quickly. "Jim was here all last night."

"Are you sure?"

"Of course," Gail said.

Eric Steffan backed that up by saying, "Maiben sat right here in the kitchen talking to me until ten o'clock. Then he bunked

140

down in the barn."

"But you can't say for certain that he didn't leave the barn," Bishop pointed out.

"Well, no," Steffan admitted. "Not for dead certain."

Gail said confidently, "I don't think North Fork entered Jim's mind at all last night. He was too concerned about the man who'd shot at him twice within a couple of hours."

Bishop nodded. "Maiben told me about that, and it's a queer thing."

"Then he went to town today," Steffan mused.

"Yes. And got into a fist fight over a woman."

"What woman?" Gail asked.

"Dulcie Wade, the one he used to go with before she got married. Soon as Maiben hit town today Ernie Wade warned him to stay away from Dulcie. But Jim looked her up just the same and they had quite a fight."

"Who won?" Gail asked.

"Maiben. He's good at fighting. Good at romancing, also. When I left town Maiben was sitting on the hotel veranda, waiting for Dulcie to get off work."

Bishop shook his head, adding glumly. "He's just asking for trouble. Next time you see Maiben you might tell him that Ernie is threatening to go after him with a gun. He's loco about that ex-wife of his'n and can't abide Maiben courting her again."

Gail revealed no sign of resentment as she stood there watching Bishop ride off. But presently, as Eric Steffan hobbled back into the kitchen, he heard her say, "Darn him, anyway!"

CHAPTER TEN

Burro Smith was a patient man. He sat alone on the hotel veranda, not taking a nip at the bottle until he reckoned the half hour was up. Then he sampled it, grunting his relish for the bourbon's fine flavor, and waited out another half hour interval. Jim Maiben, he reckoned, must have important business to keep him so long. To Burro's way of thinking there wasn't anything more important than drinking bourbon from a bottle.

Ernie Wade came along the sidewalk. He stopped in front of Burro, his battered face wearing a deep-rutted frown as he asked, "Did Maiben go into the hotel while you been sittin' here?"

"No," Burro said, keeping the bottle out of sight. "I ain't saw him all evenin'."

Ernie smelled the bourbon, for he asked, "You got a bottle?"

Burro shook his head. "Where'd I git cash

for a whole bottle of whisky?"

"Well, you smell like a distillery," Wade muttered and walked on past the hotel. Then he quartered across Main Street and stopped on the opposite sidewalk for a moment's appraisal of the thoroughfare before going into the Spur.

Burro observed that Ernie was wearing a holstered six-shooter. He tried to recall if Jim had been armed, and couldn't remember if he was or not. Better be, Burro reflected. That Ernie Wade looked loco as a pulque-drunk Yaqui. . . .

Itching for another drink, Burro held the bottle up to the window lamplight, judged its contents and decided against further sampling until Jim came back. A chill breeze stirred dust fumaroles in the street, and it reminded Burro that he was in his shirt sleeves. He was tempted to take a drink against the evening's coolness, but resisted the temptation. A man shouldn't be hoggish with sociable likker. Cradling the bottle of bourbon affectionately he went into the deserted lobby, climbed a flight of stairs and presently opened the door of room number five.

The bracket lamp had been turned low; he didn't notice Dulcie until she said, "It took you long enough."

She had been lying on the bed. Now, seeing it wasn't Jim Maiben, she sat up and hastily drew a black silk nightgown more securely across her bosom. "What are you doing here?" she demanded.

"Jim told me to come up and make myself to home," Burro said, revealing his surprise in the way he gawked at her.

"Where is Jim?"

Burro grinned, liking what he saw. He said, "Reckon he'll be along directly. Jim invited me to sleep here tonight." Burro chuckled, recalling what Jim had told him. "He said if I found anybody in the bunk to tell 'em to move over."

"You're lying!" Dulcie protested. "I know Jim Maiben wouldn't say a thing like that."

"I reckon he was just funnin' me," Burro said, wanting to pacify her. He had always liked Dulcie Todd's looks, but now he peered at her with increased admiration. "I knowed you would look sassy sweet on a bed," he announced in the slow way of a man expressing a profound conviction. "I used to think about Ernie seein' you like this every night, and I thought he was the luckiest cuss alive. Now I know it, for a fact."

Dulcie was flattered. Her lips loosened into a smile that got into her eyes, giving them a flirty look. She lifted a hand to tuck back a vagrant strand of her high-piled hair, that gesture revealing an armpit and the creamy bulge of a breast. The perfumed, woman smell of her was a tantalizing thing to Burro Smith; it roused a tingling sense of anticipation in him. Here, by grab, was the prettiest female he'd seen in many a year. The most desirable. It made him itch all over just to look at her lying there.

Dulcie said, "Jim might not like it if he finds you here with me, Mister Smith."

"Don't call me mister, ma'am," Burro suggested smilingly. "And don't fret yourself about Jim Maiben. Me and him are old friends."

He uncorked the bottle, saying, "Let's us have a drink, Dulcie. It's bourbon."

"Oh, I never touch liquor," she said, as if shocked that he should suspect she did.

That surprised Burro Smith. He'd thought all chancy females drank whisky at a time like this. They seemed to need it before they could really get loosened up and enjoy themselves. He wondered how soon Jim Maiben would arrive, and hoped it wouldn't be right away. A man didn't get a chance to be this close to a sweet-smelling woman like this very often. Placing the whisky on a commode he took out his Durham sack and asked, "Want me to roll you a cigarette?"

"I don't smoke, either," Dulcie announced. "Guess I'm just old fashioned."

Burro grinned at her. "That's the kind of women I like best," he said cheerfully. "Old fashioned."

He had thought it was good manners to fuss around a little first, but Dulcie was as much as telling him it wasn't necessary. He chuckled, thinking how this was going to be. He said, "You don't drink, and you don't smoke. Well, that makes it simple, don't it?"

Dulcie acted like she didn't understand. She watched him come toward the bed, not moving until he reached down to put his arms around her. Then she drew back and said haughtily, "I don't honeyfuss with dirty old bums, either."

Burro peered at her, puzzled as a man could be. "You funnin'?" he demanded.

"No, and I'm telling you to leave me alone."

Burro laughed at her. "Look who's actin' uppity," he jeered, and reach for her again.

Dulcie avoided his eager hands by throwing herself backward and rolling across the bed, that violent movement exposing the symmetrical voluptuousness of white thighs. Free of the bed she darted across the room and said pantingly, "You leave me be or I'll scream!"

Burro gawked at her. "You mean it?"

"Of course I do. You get out of this room."

Burro couldn't understand it. She had been waiting here for Jim Maiben, hadn't she? A woman who did that wanted to honeyfuss, and shouldn't be so damned particular about it. . . .

"You'd better get out of this room before Jim arrives," Dulcie warned. "He'll half kill you if he finds you here with me."

"That's loco," Burro disagreed. "Jim knowed you was up here, didn't he?"

She nodded.

"Well, he invited me to spend the night here. Me and Jim are real good friends. He wouldn't raise no fuss about us havin' some fun in his room."

"What do you take me for?" Dulcie demanded angrily.

Burro grinned at her. "A teaser," he said. "An itchy little teaser that needs a man real bad."

"You get out of here this instant!" Dulcie commanded in an outraged voice.

Burro shook his head. "I'm sleepin' here, honey."

He sat on the bed and took off his moccasins. "I've met some counterfeit females in my time," he reflected disgustedly. "But none so counterfeit as you."

"Your feet stink awful," Dulcie complained, holding her nose.

Burro peeled off sweat-soaked socks, revealing grimy feet. He said, "You'd stink too, if it wasn't for all that perfumery," and flung the wet socks at her.

Dulcie dodged the socks and quickly opened the door. "You damned dirty old bum!" she shrilled and ran down the hallway to her room.

Burro got up and closed the door. Women, he thought, were wholly unpredictable. Especially white women. You could never tell by looking at them. It seemed like they all wanted to be chased, but some of them didn't want to be caught. Hell of it was a feller couldn't tell which was which. How was he to know whether they meant it or not? Squaws, now, were more reasonable. If a squaw wanted a man she didn't make him go through a lot of damned monkeyshines first.

He walked over to the window and took a look at Main Street, seeing no sign of Jim Maiben. Then he went to the commode and uncorked the bottle. Jim couldn't expect him to go dry all night with good bourbon within drinking distance. Burro was tilting the bottle to his lips when the door opened behind him and Ernie Wade snarled, "Now you git it, Maiben!"

Burro peered over his shoulder, saw the cocked gun and the wildness in Wade's eyes. "I ain't Maiben!" he croaked. "Don't shoot me, Ernie!"

A surprised grunt slid from Wade's lips. He gave the room a quick, questing glance. "Where's Maiben?" he demanded.

"I don't know," Burro said. "He had to go see some feller on business."

As Wade absorbed that information, Burro turned slowly and held out the bottle.

Ernie shook his head. He peered about the room again, and said morosely, "I got to stay sober until I find Jim Maiben."

"Why you huntin' him?" Burro inquired innocently.

"None of your damned business," Ernie muttered and backed toward the doorway.

The thought came to Burro that Jim wouldn't have a chance against this loco killer. Ernie intended to shoot him down cold-turkey. Acting upon pure impulse, he tilted the bottle to his lips and took a long drink while Ernie watched him. "Best whisky I ever drank," he said cheerfully.

Ernie inhaled like a dog sniffing scent. "Smells like bourbon."

"It is," Burro acknowledged. "And smooth as silk." He placed the bottle on the commode, took out his Durham sack and began shaping a cigarette. "I dislike drinkin' alone," he mused. "Too bad you're on the wagon, Ernie."

"Who said I was on the wagon?" Wade demanded. Holstering his gun he closed the door behind him and went quickly to the commode. The drink he took lowered the bourbon almost an inch. He shuddered and wiped his lips on the back of a hand; accepting the Durham sack Burro offered, he said, "That's the best damn drink I've had in six months. All I been able to afford is that stinkin' bar likker of Finnigan s."

"That's rank stuff," Burro sympathized. "Tastes like lame mule sweat."

Presently, when Wade had downed another drink, he sat on the bed. He sniffed again; he said, "Seems like I smell perfumery," and placed his bruised nose close to the pillow. "Smells like the stuff Dulcie used to dab behind her ears."

"Lots of women use the same perfumery," Burro offered.

But Ernie exclaimed, "She's been in here with Maiben, by God!"

Burro reached for the bottle and handed it to him. "No use frettin' about females when we got all this likker to drink," he suggested.

Ernie took a long pull at the bottle. He said, "There never was another woman so pretty as my wife."

He shook his head morosely, and slumped on the bed as if weighted by the whisky he'd consumed. "You should see her in a nightgown, Burro. The lacey black one she wears. You talk about harem queens. Hell, she's got 'em all beat."

Presently, with another drink under his belt, Wade said sadly, "I lost the prettiest sweet-lovin' woman that ever got into a man's bed."

Tears came to his eyes and his voice took on a sobbing note as he described Dulcie's charms. "She had a habit of sitting up in bed and fixing her hair with both hands. Her nightgown was so flimsy you could see right through it when she was like that, with her body tight against the lacey silk. It was the damnedest sight you ever saw."

"Shouldn't wonder," Burro agreed, recalling his reaction to a similar pose. "Some women look nakeder in a nightgown like that than if they wasn't wearin' nothin'."

Ernie nodded and lay back on the bed, so drunk now that his eyes didn't focus properly, "That's how it was with Dulcie. I've saw her bare naked, but she was even more so in that nightgown. It makes me loco just to think how she looked."

"Well, why don't you go to her room right now and have yourself a looksee," Burro suggested, wanting to get shut of him.

Ernie shook his head. "She wouldn't let me in."

"Then break down the damned door. That's what I'd do, if she was my wife. I'd bust down the door and get into bed with her."

"Wouldn't do no good," Wade said morosely. "She's so pretty I couldn't lay a hand on her unless she was willin'."

CHAPTER ELEVEN

Jim Maiben climbed into saddle at first daybreak, the puffed knuckles of his right hand and a soreness along his ribs reminding him of yesterday's fight. A fool thing, he thought, two men bruising themselves over a flirty-eyed female who needed slapping down to size. Dulcie should be married to a man like Burro Smith who knew how to handle squaws; he'd show her who was boss soon enough. Maiben grinned, guessing that Dulcie had probably got told off last night. Burro wouldn't take much lip from a cheap tramp. . . .

Crossing the stageroad Maiben spent half an hour searching for fresh horse tracks. When he finally found them he discovered something else that both surprised and pleased him — a set of boot prints that exactly matched the measurements he had notched into a mesquite twig. One man had got down and evidently tightened a cinch; a man whose tracks were identical with those he'd found at Roman Six.

"So it was Bishop, or his companion," Maiben told himself.

That knowledge stirred again a feeling of astonishment that Sid Bishop should be mixed up in an outlaw deal. Maiben had never felt any great liking for the lawman, but Sid had seemed honest enough. Certainly he had shown no sign of being an outright crook. And Sid seemed too smart to get mixed up in a calf-stealing proposition. What possible profit could there be in it for him? Or for anyone else? There was no market for veal. The stolen calves would be valueless as beef for at least two years. It just didn't make sense. A calf was a grass-eating liability from the time it was weaned until it matured into marketable beef.

Shrugging off the riddle of such witless rustling, Maiben followed the horse tracks with a rising sense of anticipation. Bishop, he believed now, was the key to whatever was going on in the Barricades. That must be why George Jessop had said to watch him.

"Good old George," he mused. There had probably never been another banker like Jessop, for George had seemed more concerned with helping folks survive their financial storms than with making money. Now George was dead, and his young wife was making eyes at a lying land agent.

"Probably sleeping with him on the sly," Maiben muttered.

Where was the justice of it?

Why should a man like George Jessop be struck down by sudden death while rascals lived to a ripe old age?

What justice was there in Eric Steffan being crippled, or Jim Maiben going to jail for a crime he hadn't committed?

Was a man's fate decided by some sardonic Jester amused by the anthill of humanity? Was life just a continuous tug of war between the Jester and Lady Luck?

Maiben had wondered about that in prison, and despite his bitterness, had rejected it. There must be some other answer to the riddle of life. But now, thinking of Jessop and Steffan, he could find none. . . .

Morning's windless hush lay all across the Barricade Hills as he rode westward at a trot. Ahead of him a rabbit scurried from a clump of greasewood and went bouncing off in frantic, zig-zag flight. Half an hour later, tracing the hoofprints into the stage road, Maiben swore disgustedly. A wagon had passed here during the night — an east-

156

bound stage with a six-horse hitch, by the look of the road — and had scuffed out all sign of tracks.

Hugely disappointed, Maiben followed the road into the Barricades; he watched for sign, finding none until he came to the Roman Six turnoff. Here he discovered the tracks of a single horse, and judged they had been made some time yesterday evening.

But why, he wondered, should Sheriff Bishop or his companion have ridden toward Roman Six? Certainly not to get another shot at him, for Sid knew he was in town. Maiben was wondering about that when he rode into the dooryard.

Gail came out to the stoop and stood there, shading her eyes against morning's bright sunlight and wiping one flour-dusted hand on her apron. Her unsmiling appraisal puzzled Maiben. She looked, he thought, like a suspicious wife speculating on what her man had been up to in town.

"Thought you had left the country," she greeted.

Maiben grinned at her. "Worried about your father's shirt?"

"Who said anything about being worried?" Gail asked coolly.

Maiben pulled up beside the stoop and

looked at her with frank admiration. There was a bloom and a wholesomeness to her that he had observed in no other woman; a magnetism that made him want to reach out and touch the rounded loveliness of her bare arm. He asked in a hopeful voice, "Am I too late for breakfast, ma'am?"

That seemed to surprise her. "I thought you'd eat breakfast at the Acme Hotel," she announced. "Isn't that where Dulcie Wade works as waitress?"

Maiben nodded. "But I left town before they opened the dining room."

That didn't seem to please her either. She peered at him in the disdainful way she had at Spanish Spring, the sense of her disapproval so strong that Maiben fingered his chin and said, "Before the barber shop opened also."

"Well, there's some coffee left," Gail said. "And hot water for shaving."

Maiben rode on to the corral. He thought, She's sore about something. Was it because she suspected he'd spent the night with Dulcie? That seemed unlikely. What difference did it make to her who he romanced with? A woman that worshipped a damned land agent as she seemed to, wouldn't fret about a fiddlefooted ex-convict. Perhaps she had waited supper for him last night.

Women, he supposed, were touchy about such things. . . .

It was Eric Steffan who inadvertently suggested another reason. Telling Maiben about Sheriff Bishop's visit, the old man ended his recital by saying, "I hear you had a fist fight with Ernie Wade."

Maiben nodded, and covertly watching Gail, asked, "Did he tell you the reason?"

"The oldest reason there is for two men fighting," Steffan said. "A woman."

Maiben could detect no reaction in Gail then, nor later as she examined the wound in his shoulder. She was civil, and that was all. His shoulder, she said, was healing satisfactorily; she applied salve to keep the dry wound from breaking open. Afterward, while Maiben shaved, she busied herself with cake dough at the kitchen table. Observing a tumbled strand of sorrel hair that fell against the nape of her neck, Maiben was tempted to tuck it in place; he had to force down an impulse to step over there and take her into his arms. He thought, If the old man wasn't here, I would.

Eric Steffan asked, "How about you starting work this afternoon? I'm worried about all that mowed hay on the north forty. It should be raked up and stacked."

"Well, I want to make a little ride first,"

Maiben said, curious to know where Bishop had gone after leaving here. He considered telling Steffan about his suspicions, and decided against it. Better, he thought, to keep his secret until there was something more definite to report.

"Sheriff Bishop says that someone raided North Creek night before last," Gail reported. "He seemed to think it might have been you, but we told him it couldn't have been."

"Much obliged," Maiben acknowledged.

Why, he wondered, would anyone have raided North Fork the same day he returned?

Was Sid Bishop mixed up in that also?

Steffan said, "I have a feeling we're in for a hard winter. I'd hate to have anything happen to that hay."

As Maiben picked up his hat and went out to the stoop, Gail said to her father, "Perhaps Clyde will come tomorrow and finish the stacking."

The hopeful way she said it, as if Hatabelle's appearance was the one thing that would make her happy, disgusted Jim Maiben. How could such a woman cotton to a damned do-gooder — to a lying bastard who talked like a gospel slinger. You'd think Clyde Hatabelle was God Almighty and could do no wrong. He might mistake one man for another and send him to prison, but that wasn't important to Gail. Just a little mistake by nice, dear Clyde. . . .

Maiben didn't look at the house as he rode out of the yard. He thought, To hell with her and her old man's hay! Following a set of horse tracks that angled southwest, he crossed the trail he had followed yesterday morning, but rode in the same general direction. He wasn't surprised when the fresh tracks petered out on the same malpais slope where the others had faded.

Patiently, in the way of a hound dog seeking a lost scent, Maiben rode a long circle with his questing eyes on the ground. He glimpsed several yearlings that bore Ernie Wade's Running W, and thought that now they belonged to Bart Volpert. Near noon he came into the Running W trail and was studying its pattern of tracks when Burro Smith rode around a bend.

"Wagh!" Smith screeched. "A damned deserter!"

Maiben grinned, waiting until Smith came up to him. Then he said, "I had an errand that had to be done, Burro. It was important."

"Nothin' could be that important," Smith protested. "Not to desert a full bottle of bourbon like that."

"How was the hotel bed?"

"Fine. Just fine."

A whimsical grin creased Burro's leathery cheeks as he added, "A mite crowded, but I got some sleep after things quieted down."

"You mean Dulcie stayed all night?" Maiben demanded.

"Not her. By God you'd of thought she was the big queen bee the way she acted. Like her sweat didn't stink. She tried to talk me into leavin'. Real sassy, too, until I throwed my wet socks at her."

Burro laughed. "You never saw a madder female. She took off down the hallway like hell wouldn't have her."

Maiben joined the laughter. "I'd have liked to see that," he said. "It sort of evens up for a trick she pulled on me one time."

Then he asked, "Who'd you share the bed with?"

"Ernie Wade."

Burro pointed an accusing finger at Maiben; he said, "You damn near got me kilt. I was sittin' there havin' a spot of bourbon when in busts Ernie with a gun in his hand. I thought he was goin' to shoot me down for sure. He was so worked up he might've plugged me anyhow, except that I offered him a drink."

Burro grimaced. "Good thing you wasn't in that room or you'd been a gone goose. Ernie was all primed to kill you. After a couple drinks he started blubberin' about that ex-wife of his'n. How any growed man could git so worked up about a goddamn counterfeit female is beyond me. Why she's no better'n a parlor-house slut except that she acts fancy about it. To hear Ernie take on you'd think she was the only woman alive with female equipment."

"He's got it bad," Maiben agreed.

"Bad? Hell, Jim, he's a ravin' maniac and you'd best watch out for him. Ernie hates your guts."

Maiben nodded. He asked, "You got any ideas about who is stealing calves, Burro?"

"Them North Fork settlers, of course. Who else would eat veal?"

"You think the weanlings are being butchered?"

Burro nodded. "That's why they disappear so fast. There's a hell smear of them settlers. They've got no beef critters and don't know how to hunt themself wild meat. It looks simple as pourin' water out of a bucket, to me. Don't see how else it could be."

When Maiben rode off into the brush, Burro called, "Don't forgit what I told you

163

about Ernie Wade."

Maiben nodded, thinking now that an unplanned ride last night had probably saved his life. Lady Luck had had her arm around him. . . .

By midafternoon he was in the benchland above timberline, close to the base of West Divide. The rock outcrop here was mostly in long slabs with occasional patches of soil between them; in one of these patches he found the fresh sign of a horse and a calf. Farther on he saw what appeared to be the tracks of several calves and two horses.

Soon after that the tracks vanished on a broad area of slab rock, the only visible sign of passage being occasional scar marks where a shod horse had clawed for footing. Maiben halted and took his bearings. This, he judged, was a trifle northwest of Spanish Spring and just east of the Cathedrals, a weird region of chimney buttes rising above a jigsaw puzzle of box canyons carved deep into the granite walls of West Divide. No cattle ranged in these rocky badlands and riders seldom crossed it. Yet two men had ridden this way within the past twelve hours and there was clear sign that they had driven calves ahead of them.

Recalling how Red Pomeroy had said the calves just disappeared into thin air, Maiben thought, They're being taken through the Cathedrals.

But how?

As far as he knew every one of these canyons came to a blind end against the walls of the divide. Even if there was a canyon that could be traveled up to the rim, where would the calves go then? There wasn't any water or grass for fifty miles on the other side; nothing but desert.

Yet, despite that puzzlement, Maiben felt an exhilarating sense of achievement. He had trailed Sid Bishop into the Barricades and found the rustler trail over which stolen calves were being driven — a slab rock trail that Red Pomeroy and the others had failed to discover. Now it was just a matter of scouting these box canyons. Sooner or later he would find a patch of ground well tromped by horses and calves.

"A cinch," he told himself.

But he didn't find it that day, nor the next.

Riding into Roman Six at sundown on the third day of the searching, Maiben found Clyde Hatabelle unhitching a team from a hayrake. Hatabelle was garbed in bib overalls, with a holstered gun strapped around his waist. He smiled at Maiben and asked, "Any luck?"

Maiben shook his head, and wondered

about the gun. That, he supposed, was Steffan's idea. Or Gail's. They had probably talked Clyde into wearing it in case he was attacked by a dry gulcher. Recalling that Gail suspected Bart Volpert, Maiben smiled. There would be a pair to shoot at each other: Hatabelle and Volpert. Then, as he unsaddled his horse at the corral, another thought came to him, Sid Bishop wasn't in this deal alone. He had ridden out of town the other evening with a companion. It hadn't been Ernie Wade, who had spent the night with Burro Smith, nor did it seem likely that Sid's companion was Hatabelle. Of the men in town who might have been Bishop's companion that left Bart Volpert.

Thinking back to that afternoon, Maiben recalled the gun scabbard on Volpert's saddle. According to Mike Finnigan, Bart and Sid had been in the Spur together. Even though Volpert had ridden out of town before sundown, he could have crossed the bridge and doubled back to Bishop's house through Sabino Arroyo. . . .

Maiben threw hay to his horse and then leaned against the corral fence, thinking this out. Volpert had seemed too cautious a man to be mixed up in a range-grabbing deal against Steffan. But now it occurred to Maiben that the dry gulcher who had shot at him on two occasions had also been cautious. So goddamn cautious he'd hightailed yonderly after each attack instead of shooting it out.

Was Volpert Sid Bishop's partner?

Was Bart the man Hatabelle had seen leaving Ike Fenton's burning shack?

Maiben swore softly, remembering that Helen Rand had mistaken him for Volpert, as had Gail. If Volpert *was* the dry gulcher that would explain several things, including Steffan being wounded and the raid on North Creek. It would mean that Volpert was playing both factions against each other in a loco attempt to grab this range. But it didn't explain the disappearance of weanling calves. If Bishop and Volpert were stealing those calves what were they doing with them?

He was thinking about that as he washed up at the basin on the stoop. It still didn't seem reasonable that Bart Volpert had guts enough for such violence, yet Maiben couldn't discard the conviction that he was Sid Bishop's partner. . . .

At the supper table Hatabelle told about his progress with the haying, and Gail remarked, "It's good to have a worker on the place."

That, Maiben supposed, was her way of

saying that he was just a saddle bum who spent his time traipsing through the hills for no good purpose. Because he hadn't mentioned his suspicions about Sid Bishop, Gail probably considered his daily riding a waste of time. And that, he thought dismally, was what it amounted to; a damned useless chore.

He was sitting on the stoop after supper when Gail came to the doorway and said, "I forgot to tell you something that Sheriff Bishop said when he was here the other day. He said Ernie Wade intended to kill you if he could."

Maiben grinned. "Ernie seems to think I want his ex-wife."

"Don't you?"

"Wouldn't take her as a gift."

"You wouldn't?"

When he shook his head, she asked, "Then why did you fight over her with Wade?"

"Well, I didn't have much choice. Wade jumped me when I wasn't looking. After that it was just a case of defending myself."

Aware of Gail's continuing appraisal, Maiben said, "I didn't stay in town the other night. Camped in a dry-wash on Apache Mesa. Alone."

That explanation seemed to displease

Gail. She said sharply, "There's no reason for you telling me where you stayed, alone or otherwise. It makes no difference to me who you stay with."

"Suppose not," Maiben agreed, observing the heightened color in her cheeks and liking the way she looked now. "Wish it did."

Then, as Hatabelle joined Gail in the doorway, Maiben said, "I followed Sid Bishop out of town that night, and lost his trail. I've got reason to think he's mixed up in this calf-stealing deal."

"Why that's preposterous!" Hatabelle exclaimed. "Sid Bishop is honest as the day is long. He has worn himself out trying to catch the thieves."

"Is that so?" Maiben said dryly, and went on to the barn.

Afterward, when Hatabelle bunked down near him in the hay and asked, "You awake?" Maiben didn't answer him.

Why bother explaining something the land agent wouldn't believe?

Gail probably wouldn't believe it either. Hell, he wouldn't have accepted it himself if he hadn't seen Bishop sneak out of town through Sabino Arroyo.

Thinking of his suspicion about Bart Volpert he decided to take a look at the country around Spade tomorrow. . . .

Maiben was sleeping soundly when something roused him. He reared up in his blankets, not knowing what it was, until Cylde Hatabelle whispered, "Somebody outside called your name."

Ernie Wade, Maiben thought instantly and reached for his holstered gun. Then he heard Burro Smith call from the barn doorway, "You awake, Jim?"

"Yes, Burro. What's up?"

"Well, I took a load of wood to town and dilly-dallied around until after dark before I started home. Just before I got to the Running W turnoff Ernie Wade overtook me. Said he was goin' huntin' in the hills, but all he had was a six-gun. I think you're the one he wants, Jim. Thought I'd better warn you to be on the watch for that loco bastard."

"Much obliged," Maiben acknowledged. "I'll buy another bottle of bourbon one of these days."

As Smith rode away from the barn door, Hatabelle said sleepily, "Perhaps you'd better help me with the haying tomorrow. Nobody could sneak up on you in that big field."

"I got other plans," Maiben muttered. "Real important plans."

CHAPTER TWELVE

Ernie Wade was standing at the Spur bar, nursing the drink he'd talked Finnigan into giving him on credit, when the hotel night clerk stepped up to him and said, "Dulcie wants to see you. She's waiting on the veranda."

Ernie peered at the pimply faced clerk and asked sourly, "You funnin' me?"

The clerk shook his head. "She's real anxious to see you," he insisted.

Ernie still couldn't believe it. Dulcie hadn't so much as smiled at him for months; scarcely spoke when they met, which was seldom. He looked the clerk in the eye; he said, "By God, if you're funnin' me I'll bust you wide open!"

Then, so excited that he forgot the drink in his hand, Ernie started toward the batwings.

"Where you going with that glass?" Mike Finnigan demanded.

Ernie stopped and looked at the glass. He smiled sheepishly and said, "Forgot I had it."

"Them things cost money," Mike grumbled. "And I can't buy 'em on credit, like some folks buy their likker."

One of the men at the bar laughed out loud, and others grinned at Ernie who muttered, "You'll git your pay. Anyone would think I was bein' given free likker, the way you talk."

He downed the whisky at a gulp, deposited the glass on the bar, and hurried out of the saloon. That goddamn Mick was always making remarks like that; always rubbing it in because a customer happened to be short of cash. But presently, as Wade crossed Main Street's wide dust, he forgot his embarrassment. Why, he asked himself, should Dulcie have sent for him?

What would she want to see him about?

Many a night, lying awake in bed, he had hoped she would get as lonesome as he was, and send word for him to come to her. But he'd never really believed she would. It was just a dream; something to hope for. . . .

Ernie peered at the Acme veranda, seeing no sign of Dulcie near the window or doorway lamplight. Was that damned clerk putting a joke over on him? He glanced back at the Spur, half expecting to see grinning faces above the batwings. There was none, but when he came to the sidewalk, he still couldn't see any sign of Dulcie. It occurred to Wade now that she might have sent the message as a joke. Perhaps Jim Maiben was in town. Dulcie might be up on the front gallery, with Maiben, waiting to douse him with a dumped slop bucket. He was glancing apprehensively at the upstairs gallery when Dulcie called to him from the far end of the veranda.

It was dark where she stood, and he couldn't distinguish her facial expression as he hurried to her, but when she said, "I'm so glad you came," he was sure she was smiling.

Ernie said, "I'm glad too."

He got his arms around her quick and gave a sighing grunt as he searched for her lips; she let him kiss her, then pushed him onto the veranda bench and sat on his lap while he kissed her again.

It was a dream come true for Ernie Wade. He felt like laughing and crying at the same time. He hugged her so hard she gasped for breath. He inhaled the sweet smell of her, savoring the familiar fragrance. He kissed her ear, and the tip of her nose, and the little hollow under her chin. He said,

"Honey, honey," over and over in the crooning way he'd used to say it.

Dulcie made his hands behave. She said censuringly, "Not here, Ernie. Someone might see us."

"Then let's go upstairs," he suggested, frantic with his need for her.

"Oh, I couldn't do that."

"Why not?"

She didn't reply for a moment. Then, sadly, as if confessing a tragic and shameful thing, she said, "Jim Maiben put an evil spell on me long ago, Ernie. I can't explain it. But it's true. He has a power over me that I can't break. Except for that I'd still be your wife."

"Damn him!" Ernie exclaimed. "What did he do to you?"

Dulcie shrugged, and held tight to him, as if afraid. "It's a queer thing," she murmured. "I never loved Jim Maiben, but he has some power over me. A wicked, awful power." She sighed, and said regretfully, "I guess it'll always be that way, as long as he's alive."

"I can fix that," Ernie muttered. "I can fix him so he'll never bother you again."

"How?"

"With a gun."

Dulcie didn't say anything to that. She cuddled closer in his arms and rubbed her nose against his cheek.

"You want me to kill him?" Ernie asked.

She acted like she didn't hear him. She kept nuzzling his cheek with her nose and then with her parted lips in a way that made Ernie shiver.

He said, "There never was a woman so sweet as you, Dulcie. I'd do anything you wanted. Anything at all."

Then he asked, "You want Maiben killed?"

For an answer she found his lips and kissed him, using her lips in the way she'd done when they were first married. It drove Ernie frantic with desire. He stood up, holding her in his arms, and said gustily, "I'm toting you upstairs to a bed."

But Dulcie talked him out of it. Forcing him to put her down she said, "Not while he's alive, Ernie. I just couldn't. You'll have to wait — until afterward."

Then, pulling free of his arms, she went quickly along the veranda and into the lobby.

Ernie sat down on the bench, his heart thumping and his whole body aching. He shaped up a cigarette with trembling fingers. "She'll be my wife again," he told himself. "Just like before."

He had the odd feeling that he was dreaming; that what had happened here wasn't real at all. Yet he could still smell Dulcie's perfume; could still taste the flavor of her mouth. And his heart was pounding against his ribs as it used to when he watched Dulcie put up her hair.

She could sure stir a man up.

She could make him feel ten foot tall, and strong as a stallion.

Thinking of what she'd told him about the spell Maiben had put on her, Ernie cursed savagely. That explained everything. No wonder she had quit him. A woman couldn't be blamed for a thing like that. It was something they couldn't help; an evil, mysterious power they couldn't resist no matter how hard they tried. A hex, like the niggers used. Maybe Maiben had some nigger blood in him; maybe that's how come he could put an evil spell on a woman. Dulcie wanted to be free of it so she could be his wife again. That's why she'd sent for him.

She wanted to be free of Jim Maiben!

In all his wishing, Ernie had never hoped for that. It hadn't seemed possible that Dulcie would want Jim Maiben done away with. He could scarcely believe it, even now. She had bragged so much about him. That he supposed, was part of the hex, making a woman brag to her husband about another man. She had seemed so smitten with Maiben that it was hard to believe she wanted to be free of him now. But he had to believe it, and he had to do what she wanted.

So thinking, Ernie went to the livery stable and talked Joe Blair into lending him a horse. Then he rode to his shack and made a blanket roll of provisions, after which he rode out of Tonto Bend with a smile on his lips.

Killing Jim Maiben shouldn't be so difficult. Just a matter of watching for a sure shot. . . .

Ernie was the happiest man in Barricade Basin that night as he camped in the brush a few miles north of Roman Six. So happy that he had a difficult time getting to sleep.

It was full daylight when he awoke the next morning and cooked himself a hasty breakfast of canned beans and coffee. Eager to be on his way, Ernie stuffed his meagre equipment into the blanket roll and loped southward to a sandstone reef which gave him a good view of Steffan's place. For a few moments, as his eyes focused on the distant yard, he saw no sign of movement.

"Slept late, like me," he decided.

But a moment later he saw a man come

out of the corral with a team of horses and hitch them to a hayrake. Ernie grinned, guessing that Jim Maiben was going to Steffan's hayfield. This would make it easier than he had expected.

Ernie rubbed his nose, and recalled Dulcie's talk last night. It still didn't seem quite real to him; more like a dream. . . .

He watched the team leave the yard and said jubilantly, "You won't mess with her again, you bastard!"

Leaving the sandstone reef, Ernie rode down into brush and tied his horse to a mesquite. Then he walked out to where fresh wheel tracks showed in a trail that led northward; he crossed the trail and forted up behind a hip-high rock outcrop. Squatting here he took out his Colt and checked its load. He was less than fifteen feet from the wheel tracks. He smiled, thinking what a forty-five-caliber slug would do to Maiben at this range.

"Rip his guts to ribbons," Ernie mused.

That's what the bastard deserved — gut shooting. And that was what he'd get.

Anticipation made Ernie sweat and shiver at the same time. He stood up to peer southward. The team should be coming close. Brush obstructed his view, but now he heard a remote tromp of hoofs, that sound increasing as he listened.

Ernie crouched down again. He'd keep out of sight until the team came abreast of this outcrop. Then he would rear up and start shooting before Maiben had a chance to draw his gun. Ernie grinned, thinking that he'd be back in town before dark to tell Dulcie the good news.

The hayrake was coming close now, near enough so that Ernie could hear its high wheels turning. He cocked the gun, forcing himself to wait until the team plodded past the outcrop. Then he bobbed up, and recognizing Clyde Hatabelle on the hayrake, loosed a sighing curse.

"What you up to?" Hatabelle demanded, halting the team.

Ernie felt limp. He holstered the gun and asked, "Where's Jim Maiben?"

"He rode off at daybreak," Hatabelle said, eying him suspiciously. "Did you think I was Maiben?"

Wade nodded.

"Well, there's a law against murder, Ernie. You'd better keep that in mind."

Ernie used his shirt sleeve to wipe sweat from his face. "I wasn't intendin' to shoot Maiben," he lied. "Just wanted to warn him about fussin' with my wife. She don't want him botherin' her no more."

Then he asked, "Which way did Maiben ride?"

Hatabelle shrugged. "Didn't notice. But I wouldn't go looking for him if I was you. Jim Maiben isn't a man to fool with."

"I ain't foolin' with him none at all," Ernie muttered, and crossed the trail toward his horse. "That's what I want to tell him, so's he'll be sure to understand it."

CHAPTER THIRTEEN

It was sunup when Jim Maiben rimmed a tiptilted bench half a dozen miles northwest of Spanish Spring. Resting his horse here, Maiben reviewed the long searching which had kept him asaddle from dawn until dark each day. He had prowled countless gulches and box canyons without finding what he sought; had crossed West Divide and scouted the country beyond the Cathedrals, finding no outlet trail. But Sid Bishop and a companion had ridden into these hills by a secret route and Maiben now believed the answer might be found at Bart Volpert's ranch. So thinking he rode on across the bench and was sliding down its north edge when a rifle exploded somewhere above him.

The bullet whanged close enough to make Maiben dodge instinctively. Wheeling his horse off the bench he drew his gun; but instead of turning away from the divide,

Maiben rode toward it.

That split-second decision probably saved his life, for it brought immediate protection. Forcing his nervous horse against the high reef of rock here, Maiben listened to a continued firing that raveled out in echo fragments against canyon walls. A rifle, he decided, on some secondary shelf above this first steep barricade. Those scratching bullets laced the air above him, the angle of fire slanting them into slab rock beyond him, where lead bounced off in spanging ricochet.

Recalling that Burro had said Ernie Wade had only a six-gun, Maiben thought, This is Bishop, or Volpert, and felt a rising sense of elation. This might be the showdown — the end of all his tedious searching.

There was a belt of shadow along the talus-littered base here, and manzanita clung tenaciously to occasional dirt-filled crevices. Maiben glanced behind him, observed that there was less protection southward where the divide rose less abruptly; he eased his horse forward, keeping a sharp watch of the wall ahead. The shooting had ceased now, and he listened for sound of movement above him. He followed the divide's uneven contours seeking a canyon break that might afford an opportunity for a flank attack against the high-perched rifleman. Was it Bishop, or Volpert?

In the next instant, as another gun began blasting ahead of him, Maiben muttered: "Both of them."

And the fact that they were firing convinced him that he was close to solving the riddle of rustled calves. Even though they couldn't target him, they were trying to drive him away from here . . .

Halting to listen for sound of travel on the divide, Maiben heard a clatter of hoofs as a horse slid down some rocky incline, that sound coming from above and a trifle behind him. He wondered how the crest of the reef was along here; if a rider could reach the edge and shoot straight down at him. With that possibility in mind, Maiben moved on at a walk, tautly listening. This could be a trap if those two rimmed out close enough; he peered downslope to where the first trees were and judged them to be at least three hundred yards away. A man would make a good target riding toward them.

He was passing what seemed to be a brush-clotted recession in the granite up-thrust when he heard the clack of a shod hoof on rock, that sound seeming to be close and to his left. Maiben wheeled the bay into a pivoting turn; he peered at a thick screen of manzanita and then looked above it, detecting no break in the rock rampart.

Must've been my imagination, he thought.

A man got spooky in a deal like this. He got to hearing all sorts of things.

But now, as Maiben turned away, Sheriff Bishop said sharply "Drop that gun!"

And in the heartbeat of time that Maiben hesitated, Bishop warned, "You'll get it right between the shoulder blades!"

Maiben dropped the gun. He turned in saddle to look at Bishop who stood half hidden by manzanita, and now Bart Volpert hurried out of the brush behind him with a cocked Winchester in his hands.

Sid Bishop's frowning face was still tight with excitement, but Volpert was smiling. "So we finally caught the snooper," he said exultantly. He giggled and said to Maiben, "I missed you twice before, but I won't again."

The significance of that confession chilled Jim Maiben. It told him that here was the man who had tried to kill him twice before. The man who had burned Fenton's shack, and wounded Eric Steffan. And it told him something else: Volpert intended to kill him now!

"You once called me a chicken-livered

coward because I wouldn't run Fenton off," Volpert said, his voice chuckling with satisfaction. "You said I was a gutless gentle Annie."

He laughed, and winked at Sid Bishop who grinned back at him. They were, Maiben thought, wholly pleased with themselves. His return to Barricade Basin had worried them, but they weren't worried now.

"I had a better idea in mind than to run Fenton off," Volpert explained. "A way to get his place cheap, and own it legally. I knew nobody would suspicion me. They all thought the same as you — that I didn't have guts enough to burn a nester's shack."

Maiben shrugged. He said scoffingly, "That didn't take guts. Any sniveling kid with a match could've done it."

"Don't get sassy!" Bishop warned, waggling his Winchester threateningly. "You always was one to be talking when you should've been listening."

"Talked himself right into Yuma Prison," Volpert agreed. He moved out in front of Maiben and stood there with his rifle cocked. He said, "I started out in these hills flat broke, the same as you. But I stepped around real quiet while you talked loud and acted big. I used my head while you used your fists. Well, things are different now. I

185

own three places and will own others, including the one that belonged to you."

"How?" Maiben asked. "How'll you get the other places?"

Volpert chuckled, hugely enjoying this. He said to Bishop, "You tell him, Sid. Real simple, so's he'll understand it."

Bishop's smiling acceptance of that suggestion was a sickening thing to Jim Maiben; a servile, shameful thing for a man who wore a sheriff's badge pinned to his vest.

"Well, it's like this," Bishop said. "Cow outfits depend on their calf crops to grow into beef for marketing. Otherwise they go broke. If there's no calves there's no steers later on to sell. Simple, ain't it?"

Maiben understood that well enough, but he asked, "What good are weanling calves to you?"

Volpert winked at Bishop again. He said braggingly, "That's the part that's had 'em all guessing. And it's the best part of my scheme. I hold the calves until they're yearlings, then turn them back onto the places I've bought at bargain prices. Ernie Wade didn't have twenty calves on his place a year ago, but now there's upwards of forty yearlings on it. And they belong to me."

So that was it. That was where the profit could be gained from stolen weanling calves.

A double profit, for the loss of the calves made it possible to obtain bankrupt ranches at bargain prices. . . .

For a moment, as Maiben absorbed that information, Volpert and Bishop watched him in silence; the impersonal silence of executioners contemplating a condemned man. Then Bishop asked, "What now, Bart?"

The way Sid spoke, and the meek expression on his face, was a revelation to Jim Maiben. Here was a man who seemed so used to taking orders that he made no pretense of sharing the responsibility of decision.

"We'll take a little ride," Volpert said. "Go get the horses."

Bishop stepped obediently through the brush, and now Maiben understood that the manzanita screened a low, arched entrance into what undoubtedly was the mouth of a big canpon — a hidden, spring-watered canyon that had been turned into a secret pasture for stolen calves. Here, then, was the passageway he had been seeking; the exact spot where calves disappeared "into thin air."

But surprising as that knowledge was, it seemed less fantastic than the realization that Bart Volpert was capable of the brazen thievery and violence that had filled the secret pasture with stolen stock. Spade's owner had always been so meek in his dealings with other men; so seemingly afraid of trouble in any form. Even though Maiben had suspected Volpert last night, this confirmation of his suspicion shocked him more than the knowledge that Sid Bishop was a conniving fraud.

"You look like you're a trifle surprised," Volpert suggested.

Maiben nodded. "Didn't think you had guts enough to shoot at a man, even from ambush. I thought you were a jackrabbit. But you turn out to be a coyote."

"You mean a fox, don't you?" Volpert corrected. "A sly fox that's smart enough to get what he wants. I was never much of a hand to fight. And not much good with a gun. I should've chopped you down that first day while you were honeyfussing with Steffan's daughter. By the time she left it was too dark for accurate shooting."

"You didn't miss me by much," Maiben muttered.

He took out his Durham sack and thought, There'll never be a better chance. Probably no chance at all after Sid Bishop came out of the canyon. They intended to take him somewhere and shoot him. No doubt of that. This was his last chance for survival. But he waited a moment longer, opening the sack and deciding how to do what had to be done.

Volpert stood no more than six or seven feet in front of him, confident as a man could be. If there was some way to spook Bart into shifting his gaze for a moment. . . .

Maiben considered tossing the Durham sack at him, and decided against it. For even though Volpert's attention might be momentarily attracted to the sack, he would be looking this way. And that rifle was cocked.

Hearing hooftromp beyond the brush, and knowing how little time was left, Maiben put the sack into his pocket. Then he peered beyond Volpert and exclaimed, "Red — you're just in time!"

In this same instant, as Volpert glanced over his shoulder, Maiben spurred the bay toward Volpert and knocked him down. Bart's gun exploded, the bullet ricocheting off rock as the bay charged past Spade's sprawling owner.

The first hundred yards seemed the worst to Jim Maiben. The bay had tried to avoid colliding with Volpert; fighting his head as Maiben forced him into Volpert, the gelding had cross-fired into excited lunging and seemed to take a long time reaching full stride. Actually it was a matter of seconds, but in that fleeting interval Maiben's back muscles crawled with flinching expectation. He was halfway to timber when the first bullet slashed past him. After that, with the bay running wide open, Maiben loosed a gusty sigh each time he heard the whanging passage of a slug.

He thought with grim fatalism, the ones you hear don't hurt!

Both rifles were going now, those reports echoing flatly against the divide's high ramparts. A bullet ricocheted off a boulder so close to Maiben that a fragment of lead, or rock, slashed his right cheek. A moment later he heard the meaty slap of a bullet striking his horse. The bay squealed and swerved so sharply that Maiben tipped far out of saddle; he was clinging to the horn, attempting to pull himself back, when another slug ripped through the saddle fork and gouged hide from the bay's neck.

"Close," Maiben muttered. "Too goddamn close."

He fought the frenzied horse onto a direct course toward the trees. Peering ahead he calculated the distance now as not more than a hundred yards, and believing the bay wasn't seriously wounded, felt a rising sense of exaltation. Once he got into timber there would be a fifty-fifty chance. Well, not quite that good, considering he had no gun. But at least some chance.

They'd had him dead to rights. Helpless as a man could be. But he'd got away!

Lady Luck had her arm around him again. He said jubilantly, "Hold me tight, gal — hold me tight!"

There was a lull in the firing now. Bishop and Volpert were reloading, he supposed, and then they'd come after him hell-bent. Aware that the bay was shortening stride, Maiben gave him the spurs. But the bay didn't respond, and now, crouching low above his sweat-drenched withers, Maiben observed the bloody froth that spray back from the animal's mouth.

The first bullet had gone deep.

The bay was dying on its feet. Shortening stride at each jump.

Maiben kicked free of the stirrups; made ready to leap from saddle. Those protecting trees were at least fifty yards away. Too far for a man on foot. He cursed, knowing he couldn't run that far fast enough to survive.

The bay was floundering badly now. But he didn't go down. He kept on for another ten yards. And another ten, the bloody spray tinting the soapy lather of sweat on his shoulders.

"Good pony!" Maiben praised, and let the brave-hearted horse rate himself without urging.

The bay made it into timber traveling at a slow, short-striding lope that seemed almost mechanical, as if propelled by some indomitable thrust of courage that would not allow him to quit. The rifles were blasting again, but the range was farther now, and Maiben knew he had a chance.

Dropping off the floundering bay he ran toward a windfall, and crouching behind the dirt-crusted webbing of dislodged roots, heard the bay's labored breathing as it kept on through the trees.

CHAPTER FOURTEEN

Bart Volpert was just getting to his feet when Sheriff Bishop rode out of the canyon with a led horse. Dazed by the fall, Bart rubbed his right shoulder and muttered, "He rode me down."

Then, as full realization came to him, Volpert snatched up his rifle and triggered a shot at Maiben's retreating shape. He cursed, and fired again, his pock-pitted cheeks black with rage.

Sid Bishop had sheathed his rifle when he went after the horses. In the moment it took him to yank it from saddle scabbard, Volpert screeched, "Shoot at him, you fool! Can't you see he's getting away!"

Sid got his gun up and began firing. He saw Maiben's horse swerve sharply and then begin floundering. "The bronc is hit!" he shouted.

But the horse kept on while they emptied their rifles at that fading target.

Reloading with frantic haste, Volpert raged, "We've got to catch that son-of-a-bitch. He knows too goddamn much!"

"Sure," Sid agreed. "But how'd he get away from you, and him unarmed?"

"Rode me down, by God!" Volpert explained. "Tricked me into looking over my shoulder and jumped that damned horse right into me. I never saw such luck as Maiben has. The most witless luck a man could have."

He fired twice as Maiben galloped into timber, then snatched the reins of the led horse and vaulted into saddle.

Spurring along beside him, Bishop said confidently, "He won't get far on a hurt horse, and with no gun. We'll have him chopped down in a jiffy."

But minutes later, when they found the dead bay gelding, there was no sign of Maiben. . . .

"He's hiding out in one of these thickets," Bishop predicted. "Couldn't of gone far afoot. Just a matter of flushing him out of the brush."

Volpert agreed with that, the shift in his thinking revealed in the calm and confident way he began circling through the trees. This was the kind of game he liked: stalking a target without fear of being shot at. It stirred a sort of sensual ecstacy in him, so that each moment of delay prolonged the pleasure of anticipation. He was heading toward a windfall when Ernie Wade came riding up and demanded, "What was all that shootin' I heard a bit ago?"

"We're hunting a skunk," Volpert said.

And now Bishop called, "You see anything of a man on foot, Ernie?"

Wade shook his head, asked, "Who?"

"A real good friend of yours. Sort of shirt-tail relations, in fact."

"Relations?" Ernie asked, baffled. "I ain't got no kinfolk in these hills."

"He's related to you by marriage," Bishop explained, enjoying this. "Him and you cotton to the same woman."

"You mean Maiben?"

Bishop nodded, and now Volpert said impatiently, "Give us a hand looking for him, Ernie."

Wade grinned. "Been looking for that bastard since sunup," he admitted. "Damned near shot Clyde Hatabelle by mistake, thinkin' he was Maiben."

Then he asked, "What you after him for?"

That question stumped Sid Bishop, but Volpert said without hesitation, "Calf stealing."

Ernie gawked at him. "You mean you

195

ketched Maiben stealin' one of your calves?"

"We caught him and two other thieves running off five head of Spade calves. The other two got away, but we shot Maiben's horse out from under him."

Ernie was baffled as a man could be. "How could Maiben of been mixed up in the calf stealin' if he was in jail?"

"Well, I can't figure it out either," Volpert admitted. He glanced at Sid Bishop inquiringly and asked, "What does it look like to you, Sid?"

Bishop gave his attention to shaping up a cigarette. "No way of knowing for sure," he said slowly, taking time to think this out. "But I suspect that Maiben engineered the calf stealing for revenge, while he was in Yuma."

"That's it!" Volpert exclaimed, smiling now. "It's plain as day. Maiben was sore at all of us when he left this country. He figured a way to take out his spite on us. Probably fixed up the deal with some convict that was getting out of prison, telling him how easy it could be done, us being small outfits and all. Then he got out himself and came back to take charge personally."

"Well, I'll be damned," Ernie mused. "Then he's to blame for me selling my ranch. It was his thieves that scairt Dulcie into makin' me sell my place to you."

Volpert nodded and continued on toward the windfall, saying, "Help us find him, Ernie. And shoot on sight if you see him."

"Don't worry none about that," Ernie assured. "Nothin' would please me more than to empty this gun into that bastard."

He held his pistol poised as he circled through the trees. This, by God, was perfect. He could kill Maiben without fear of law reprisal. He peered through the pines and scouted each thicket he came to with a muscle-cocked eagerness. All the regret and black dispair of recent months focused into a tight core of impatience to get this job done and hurry back to town. It shouldn't take long, with Maiben afoot.

Ernie had only one worry now: that Volpert or Bishop would get to Maiben first. He spurred his horse into a trot, rode through a thicket of saplings and then headed for another. If he found Maiben now he could be in Tonto Bend soon after dark. Ernie smiled, thinking that he might share a bed with Dulcie tonight. . . .

CHAPTER FIFTEEN

A dozen times that afternoon, Jim Maiben believed he was a goner. Perched in the windfall where its heavily branched top lodged against another tree, he had witnessed Ernie Wade's arrival, so near to him and the others that he heard their conversation distinctly. Once, when a squirrel scampered up the windfall's slanting trunk and Ernie glanced up at it, Maiben thought sure Wade would see him. But he didn't, and now, as dusk's powder blue shadows deepened through the timber, Maiben had heard no rumor of searching riders for over an hour.

The explanation Volpert and Bishop had patched up between them for Ernie's benefit seemed too fantastic for belief; their lies so obvious that anyone should recognize the fakery. Maiben had been astonished at Wade's acceptance of that story. Yet now, remembering how he had scoffed at Gail's first suspicion about Volpert, Maiben realized that others might share Ernie's acceptance of those lies. Perhaps the trumped-up story would sound less fantastic than the truth, for who'd believe that Volpert and Bishop were drygulcher thieves intending to take over the Barricade Hills range? Folks considered Volpert a peace-loving man, and it would take more than the word of an ex-convict to convince them that Sid Bishop was other than the benevolent lawman he'd seemed to be all these years.

Yes, Maiben thought morosely, they'd believe Volpert's lies against an ex-convict. He was in ill-repute already. They'd call him a trouble-maker because of his fight with Ernie; they'd believe he had a grudge against cowmen and settlers alike. The need for vengeance had reared in him like a noxious weed the day he left Tonto Bend manacled to Sheriff Bishop. He had hated them all; all the gawking people who'd stood watching on Main Street as he followed Bishop out to the stagecoach. He had made no secret of that. . . .

So now the story would be passed all across Barricade Basin that Jim Maiben had been caught stealing calves, and that his outlaw confederates were on the loose.

Visualizing how it would be, Maiben could imagine what the wild rumors and reports would be; the exaggerations. "A bad one," they'd say in Tonto Bend. "A jailbird who's turned into a killer thief."

Where, Maiben wondered, were Wade, Bishop and Volpert now?

Three guns against an unarmed man, and they'd blast on sight of him.

Wade, he supposed, was as near to being loco as booze and frustration could make a man. Volpert and Bishop, realizing what his survival might mean, would be itching for a target. They were probably searching the country toward Roman Six, believing he would head that way. One of them might be already there, waiting to get a shot at him when he came in.

Maiben rubbed the numbness from cramped leg muscles. Lady Luck had been with him so far. But he couldn't remain up here permanently. Sooner or later he had to start walking toward water and food, a gun and a horse. Those were the basic necessities a fugitive must have. Maiben wondered if Spanish Spring was being watched. It would be a natural place for a hunter to lay in wait. All hunted things went to water eventually; animals or men, they had to have water in order to survive.

He was thirsty now, as he began easing down the tree trunk. But he understood that he couldn't go to Spanish Spring. Nor toward Roman Six. Where he would go, Maiben wasn't sure; only that it wouldn't be to either of those places.

Halfway to the ground Maiben checked his downward sliding. For a tense moment he wasn't sure what he had heard. Clinging to the rough-barked tree trunk he listened intently. Not a sound. The forest was absolutely still. No twitter of roosting birds in nearby trees; no chattering of squirrels. Too still, Maiben realized, Something was wrong. Then the muted footfalls of a horse walking on pine needles came to him, that sound near and to the south.

Maiben tightened his hold on the steep-tilted trunk, all his senses strained to sharp attentiveness. He was well below the protection of branches; he thought, Perched like a monkey on a stick, and understood there'd be no chance of escape if that oncoming rider glimpsed him now.

Hang on, and hope. Grip the dead pine hard. Sweat and shiver while your guts ache, while dread climbs into your throat so you can taste it; while the Sardonic Jester plays his game with Lady Luck. . . .

The rider stopped again, so near that

Maiben heard a bit chain rattle as the horse moved its head. Keening the dusk's deep shadows Maiben tried to locate the rider who was now moving, and saw an obscure shape pass between two high-branched pines.

Was it Volpert, or Bishop or Wade?

The man halted his horse and sat listening for what seemed an endless interval of dead silence; then he rode on, passing from Maiben's sight almost at once.

The tension ran out of Maiben in a gusty sigh. So they were still hunting him near where they'd last seen him. Or one of them was. Reckoning how it would be, Maiben supposed they'd keep on circling. Backtracking. Watching and listening. He wondered if any of them had gone to Roman Six; if Clyde Hatabelle had joined the chase. He cursed, thinking that the land agent would consider it his duty as an upright citizen. Then there'd be four guns against him. If this thing lasted long enough the North Creek settlers would get in on it. They'd welcome a chance to hunt down Jim Maiben, with orders to shoot him on sight. It would be a Roman Holiday for those damned plow jockeys. . . .

Maiben waited out a full five minutes without moving. Volpert, he decided, was smart enough to know that a man couldn't walk to Roman Six in less than three or four hours while keeping out of sight. Spade's owner would concentrate the search at this end for a while yet.

With that reasoning strong in him, Maiben slid down the tree and crouched against its upturned flange of earth-webbed roots. He wondered if Volpert or Bishop had picked up his discarded gun, and supposed they had. Even if they hadn't there'd be little chance of locating it now. It would be full dark by the time he walked back to the divide, and there was no way to pick out the secret canyon's entrance without seeing the reef's markings.

Maiben considered his chances of reaching Roman Six, and understood they weren't worth risking. He cursed, seeing no way of avoiding eventual capture. Bart Volpert wouldn't spare himself nor his companions; Spade's owner would continue the search until he found the man he was looking for. The man who knew too much. . . .

A gentle evening breeze stirred the high pines to a soft sighing. Off to the south a cow set up a continued bawling, that lonely sound prowling the pines in long echoes. The cow, Maiben supposed, was calling for a calf now hidden in Volpert's secret pasture.

Her plaintive summons was a symbol of one man's greed; a greed that already had brought ruin to the Barricade Hills.

Recalling Volpert's brag that he owned three ranches and would own others, Maiben marveled at the perfection of his strategy. Bart had left nothing to chance. Each move in his nefarious scheme had been prepared in advance. Intent on complete conquest, he had somehow manipulated a marriage with Grace Bishop which insured a sheriff's obedient co-operation. The whole thing was fantastic. Yet so damned simple. Just a matter of snatching a few calves here and there, again and again, month after month. Most of the stealing, Maiben supposed, had been done at night; but even if Volpert and Bishop were seen riding the range no one would suspect them. It would be taken for granted they were searching for stolen calves or chasing thieves.

"An air-tight proposition," Maiben muttered.

He stepped away from the windfall and scanned the darkness about him. He considered going to look for the gun, and decided there was no use. The important thing was to get some place where Volpert wouldn't be apt to search for him. That, and water. And food, if possible. After that he must figure some way of getting a horse. It was bad enough to be unarmed, but to be afoot also was next to hopeless.

But where could he go?

Not to Roman Six which was closest. Nor to Alamo Rand's, which lay in the same direction. Red Pomeroy's place was at least twenty miles from here, and Ernie Wade's old ranch nearly as far. Burro Smith might not be able to lend him a horse, but he'd furnish a grulla mule. And a gun. That, Maiben thought, would be a good joke on Volpert — his being armed, fed and mounted by a man in Bart's employ. But it was so damned far to walk. . . .

Abruptly then an idea came to Maiben; a place where Volpert wouldn't expect him to go.

"Spade," he said, and for the first time this day was thoroughly pleased with himself.

It wouldn't occur to Volpert that he would seek sanctuary at Spade. There'd probably be a horse or two in the corral. Maiben grinned, thinking that he might even talk Grace Volpert into giving him something to eat. She would have no way of guessing he was being chased by her husband.

Spade lay five or six miles northeast of this timbered slope. That way Maiben walked through pine-scented darkness.

Gail Steffan was washing the supper dishes when she heard a rider come into the yard. Thinking it was Jim Maiben she pushed the coffeepot to the front of the stove and said fretfully, "About time." But a moment later she heard Clyde Hatabelle ask, "What you doing here at this time of night, Ernie?"

Going out to the stoop where her father sat with Hatabelle, Gail saw Ernie Wade sitting his horse in the doorway's shaft of lamplight and heard him announce: "I been helping Sheriff Sid chase a rustler. He's somewhere betwixt here and West Divide — on foot."

"Who is he?" Eric Steffan demanded.

"Jim Maiben."

"Jim Maiben!" Steffan echoed. "Are you drunk?"

Ernie shook his head. "That's how it sounded to me, at first. But not after Bart Volpert and Sid explained things. They caught Maiben dead to rights with a couple other thieves, runnin' off Spade calves. Maiben's horse was shot from under him."

"That's silly," Gail protested. "Jim is no rustler. Why, that's what he's been doing for almost a week — looking for rustlers."

Ernie shook his head. "Maybe that's what

he told you, ma'am. But he's bossin' the whole deal hisself. It won't sound so loco when you hear the whole story."

"What story?" Hatabelle asked.

"Well, accordin' to Sheriff Sid and Bart Volpert, Maiben must've schemed up the calf stealin' deal while he was in prison. He had these two jiggers runnin' it for him until he got out of jail, and then he took charge."

"That's stupid, and ridiculous," Gail scoffed. She laughed at Ernie, adding, "How could you believe such a far-fetched story?"

"Because I know Maiben," Ernie muttered, anger staining his bruised face. "He's a natural-borned renegade. A Texas tough that never neighbored much with the rest of us, or cared a damn what he done, just so it pleasured him. He always was a triflin' man with women, and still is. He put some kind of a hex on Dulcie. A man that would do a thing like that would steal calves, or anythin' else. And he hated our guts when he went to prison. All of us."

Clyde Hatabelle turned to Gail now. He said thoughtfully, "Perhaps it's not so far-fetched as it sounds. Ernie is right when he says Maiben hated most of us for sending him to Yuma. Look how he greeted me, that first night. Afterward, when I tried to explain my side of it to him, he laughed at me. It's possible that he met a cow thief or two in Yuma. That's where most of them wind up. Perhaps it explains what has been going on all these months."

"Of course it does," Ernie agreed. He pointed to Steffan's crippled leg; he said harshly, "You bein' shot was Maiben's fault, even if he didn't do it hisself. And so was me losin' my ranch."

Gail shook her head. "I don't believe it," she said quietly. "I just don't believe that Jim Maiben is a thief."

Hatabelle peered at her. "Do you know him well enough to judge?" he asked, and in the moment while Gail thought about that, added, "Maiben had a wild streak in him even before he went to prison. He was a good hater then, and three years in Yuma made him worse. I wouldn't put anything past him."

"But he was shot at the day he came back," Gail pointed out. "How do you explain that?"

Hatabelle shrugged. He glanced at Ernie and asked, "Did you know Maiben was being released from prison?"

"Sure, same as everybody else in town," Wade admitted.

"Were you the one who welcomed him home with a bullet?"

"Who, me? Hell no. I didn't even know he was back till I saw him in the Spur."

Gail smiled. She asked, "So how do you explain that, Clyde? And the horse tracks Jim found in this yard the next morning?"

Hatabelle shrugged again. "It's a mixed up mess, for a fact," he admitted.

"It is that," Eric Steffan agreed soberly. "And Gail may be right about Maiben, Clark. Women have a way of knowing such things. It is hard to fool a woman."

Ernie Wade wasn't interested in conversation. He was hungry and now called Gail's attention to that fact by asking, "Could I have a cup of coffee, ma'am? Ain't ate nothin' since breakfast."

"Of course," Gail agreed, and presently, as Wade sat down at the table, she asked, "Where are Volpert and Bishop?"

"Out in the brush, searchin' for Maiben. Which is where I'll be soon as I finish eatin'. That dirty son needs killin' for what he done to Dulcie, and I'd like to be the one that does it."

"What did he do to her?" Gail asked.

"Put a hex on her, that's what he done. Made her quit her own husband even when he was in jail, so's she'd be waitin' for him when he got out. Dulcie didn't want to talk to him the day he come back, but she just couldn't help herself. Maiben had a power over her."

Gail nodded, seeming to agree. She said softly, "The power of male attraction, and a sort of animal magnetism."

Ernie gawked at her. "You too?" he demanded. "Did Maiben use it on you, too?"

Gail nodded and smiled at him. "But it's no hex, Ernie. It's the physical attraction some men have for some women."

She watched him devour his warmed-up supper, thinking that Jim Maiben was going hungry. She said, "You shouldn't blame Maiben for the fact Dulcie left you. She's old enough to know what she's doing."

Ernie went on eating as if he hadn't heard.

Gail said insistently, "And Jim had nothing to do with the calf stealing. That's just something Bart Volpert made up."

"Makes no difference to me, one way or the other," Ernie muttered. "It's what he done to Dulcie. That's what I'll kill him for."

CHAPTER SIXTEEN

It was a long walk. A slow, stumbling walk during which Jim Maiben thought of many things: of Gail Steffan's belief that Clyde Hatabelle would not lie, and her insistence that Bart Volpert was the man whose treachery had sent him to prison. Recalling how sure she had been, Maiben wondered why her suspicion had not impressed him; why he had rejected it as being a huge joke. It didn't seem comical now, by God.

Maiben cursed, realizing that his mind had been so clotted with a need for vengeance that he hadn't been able to think straight. But he could think straight now, and he understood that no matter what happened from here on out, all he would win was survival. Nothing more. Even if he somehow managed to reach Tonto Bend, who would believe him?

Not Joe Blair who feared reprisal. Nor Mike Finnigan. Nor Dutch Elmendorf. Not

Sam Meaker who had used a wife and three little girls as a shield against an expected bullet. Clyde Hatabelle might believe him, because of Gail's influence. Gail and her father, having suspected Volpert all along, would probably believe him. But not the others.

Remembering how hugely Gail's responsive lips had roused him, Maiben thought about her marrying Hatabelle. He visualized how it would be with her for a wife; how completely she would reward a husband. There was in Gail a priceless blending of warmth and serenity and graciousness that went beyond the oval loveliness of her face or the shapeliness of her body; a magic merging of full-blooded vitality with the modesty of a proud and sensitive woman. She had a quality that was like the inherent dignity of a queen, yet beneath that composure was all the turbulence of a woman who would bring a flood-tide of affection to the man of her choice. Comparing that reward with what was in store for him, if he survived this deal — a drifter's aimless existence — Maiben cursed morosely. And although he no longer hated Clyde Hatabelle, there was no way of quelling the embers of jealousy that burned in him.

It was less dark when he left the timber. Starlight gave the mesquite-blotched flats a faint illumination. Topping a rock outcrop Maiben glimpsed the lighted windows of Spade, and spent five minutes scouting the roundabout terrain for sign of movement. There was none, and now, as he walked toward the ranch house, he concentrated on the chore ahead of him. The most important thing was to obtain a horse, but because he had eaten nothing since breakfast and was ravenously hungry, supper ranked a close second. Thinking back to his casual acquaintance with Grace Bishop he felt confident that she would feed him. Grace had been somewhat shy as a girl; motherless for years — she had fairly worshipped her father and seemed content to keep house for him while other girls traipsed off to attend high schools at Tucson or El Paso.

Coming close to the yard, Maiben observed that only the kitchen was lighted, its door open and Grace sitting on the stoop. The thought came to him that this must be a lonely life for her, and he marveled that she had married Bart Volpert. What had she seen in him? The man was far from being handsome. Bart possessed none of the cavalier traits that women admired. Yet she had married him, and jilted Red Pomeroy who was young and reasonably handsome. It didn't seem to make sense at all.

Maiben stood near the corner of Volpert's corral long enough to distinguish the obscure shapes of four horses in the dark enclosure and to satisfy himself that Grace was alone. Then, so as not to frighten her, he called, "Hello the house!"

Grace stood up at once; she peered across the lamplit yard and asked nervously, "Who is it?"

"Jim Maiben," he said, and stepped out where she could see him. "Lost my horse back yonder and came over to borrow one."

Grace thought about that for a moment before saying, "Well, I suppose Mr. Volpert wouldn't mind."

Then, as if this might make a difference, she added, "But there's no saddle."

"I'll ride bareback," Maiben assured her, "and be real glad to do it."

Now, walking up to where she stood, he was shocked by the change in this girl's appearance since he had last seen her. Grace looked ten years older. She had always been a pretty girl. A trifle on the thin side, perhaps, but pretty in the face. And neat about her appearance. Now her hair was carelessly braided in pigtails, and a soiled gingham dress hung on her like a sack. But the greatest change was in her face, which was oddly devoid of expression — the face of a woman feeling neither pleasure nor resentment at this intrusion; feeling nothing at all. And her dark eyes held the dull, beaten look of a blanket squaw.

She asked, "Will you have something to eat?"

"Yes, ma'am, if it won't be too much trouble."

"Well, Mister Volpert didn't come home to supper, so there's plenty to warm up."

The way she said "Mister Volpert" you'd think she was speaking of an employer, instead of her husband, Maiben thought. He said, "I'll go catch a horse while you're putting supper on."

With the aid of lighted matches he found an old bridle hanging on the wagonshed wall, and slipped it on the first horse he was able to corner in the corral. The fact that Volpert kept up a saddleband of horses in his corral should have made folks suspicious, Maiben reasoned. It showed Bart was doing more riding than a man ordinarily did. But few visitors ever came to Spade, he supposed; certainly not Red Pomeroy or Eric Steffan. He tied the horse to a gate post and stood listening for a long moment before going to the house. It wasn't likely that Bart Volpert would show up here tonight, but there was no telling what a squirmy drygulcher would do. . . .

Grace Volpert watched Maiben eat without speaking. It was as if his being here meant nothing to her, one way or the other; except for the pallor of her face and its delicately formed features, she was squawlike as a woman could be. It seemed beyond belief that marriage could have changed her so much in so short a time.

Ordinarily Jim Maiben would have been well pleased with himself for having acquired a meal at Volpert's table; would have felt a secret exultation as he ate the food of his absent host. But there was something wholly depressing about this young wife who looked so dull and hopeless. What, he wondered, had Volpert done to her? How much brutality and abuse had it taken to alter her so radically? And why had Sid Bishop allowed his daughter to reach this state of haglike degradation?

Grace got up and poured Maiben a second cup of coffee. Presently she asked, "Have you seen Red Pomeroy since you got back?"

Maiben nodded, whereupon she asked, "How is he?"

For a brief interval then, as he described Pomeroy's appearance, her eyes brightened

216

with interest and a faint animation came to her face. Afterward she said, "Next time you see Red please tell him I couldn't help it. Tell him I had to marry Mister Volpert."

"Had to?" Maiben demanded.

Grace nodded.

"Why?"

Grace shook her head. "It's a secret," she murmured, the dullness coming back into her eyes. "A terrible secret that can never be told."

Moved more by pity for this dejected girl than by curiosity, Maiben said, "Well, you could tell me, Grace. I'm good at keeping secrets, and maybe I can help you somehow."

She shook her head. "Nobody can help me," she whispered hopelessly.

For a time she seemed lost in the dark pit of her loneliness. Her blankly gazing eyes peered at the table's oil-cloth and she seemed oblivious of Maiben's presence. It reminded him of the way convicts sat in their cells staring blankly at the floor.

"I know how it is to be lonesome," Maiben said.

Grace peered at him with a fresher interest. As if recognizing an important fact she said, "Yes, you've been in prison. You know what it means."

Maiben nodded. Sensing a sympathetic attitude in the way she looked at him now, he said meekly, "I'm an ex-convict and most folks don't like that. They look the other way when they meet me on the street."

Grace thought about that while he finished his coffee. Finally she said, "It must be awful, being shut up in a prison. I guess it would kill my father, even if they didn't hang him. Just being in prison would kill him."

That reasoning kindled a swift suspicion in Maiben. "So that's why you married Volpert," he mused. "On account of your father."

Grace nodded. "I intended to marry Red Pomeroy. He was the only man I ever so much as looked at." A wistful smile changed her lips as she remembered how it had been. "He was so nice to me. Red always shaved and slicked up when he came to court me. I guess there isn't a nicer man anywhere than Red. He's so gentle, and kind."

"Red felt real bad about you marrying Volpert," Maiben said.

Grace nodded again, frowning with self reproach. "It was an awful thing to do, me being promised to him and all. I wanted to explain it to Red, but Mister Volpert wouldn't let me talk to him, or anybody

218

else. He said if he ever caught me talking to a man he'd horsewhip me."

She grimaced, adding, "He did once, for visiting Gail Steffan. He used a buggy whip on me."

"The dog," Maiben muttered. "The dirty stinking dog."

"Oh, you mustn't call him that!" Grace protested. "I am his wife. His legal married wife. You shouldn't say such things to a man's wife. It's not fitting."

That shocked Jim Maiben. It seemed worse, somehow, than her recital of Volpert's brutality. He said, "And they fought a war to free negro slaves."

Grace peered at him questioningly. "Mister Volpert never kept negro slaves," she announced, as if this was one thing she could be proud of. "He's from a northern state which didn't believe in slavery."

"Good for him," Maiben said sarcastically. "Good for nice, kind Mister Volpert. But you should leave him, Grace, and never come back. No wife has to stay with a husband who horsewhips her."

Grace stared at him in disbelief. "You mean run away and never come back."

Maiben nodded. Thinking of the horses in the corral, he suggested, "You can ride with me tonight and we'll go to Tonto Bend, or anywhere you say. Just so you get away from here."

"Oh no. I couldn't do that. Mister Volpert would tell everyone about my father, and he'd go to prison."

"For what?"

"For killing a man in Texas," Grace explained sadly. "It happened a long time ago, but Mister Volpert knows about it. That's why I had to marry him. And it's why —"

Maiben saw her eyes dilate. He saw her cheeks go chalky with fright. For one confused moment he thought she was staring at him. Then, as she loosed a piercing scream, Maiben understood that she was looking at the open window behind him.

Volpert, he thought instantly.

No one else would frighten her so much.

Volpert had outguessed him!

Yet even now, with that knowledge rifling through him, Maiben didn't turn around. Gripping his coffee cup he glanced at the lamp.

"Smart, ain't you!" Volpert called from the window. "Thought I wouldn't expect you to come here. Well, I'm a trifle smarter than you figured, Maiben. Smarter than you'll ever be."

Maiben shrugged, not moving until he heard Volpert lift a leg over the window sill.

Then he pitched the cup at the lamp and dove toward the doorway.

The shattering of the lamp globe and the blast of Volpert's gun merged into one smash of room-trapped sound. But Jim Maiben didn't hear it. He was remotely aware of a tremendous impact against his right temple, and a brief bloom of weirdly darting lights that blinded him. After that, for a time, there was nothing at all.

Ernie Wade's departure from Roman Six was the signal for a half hour of earnest conversation between Gail Steffan and Clyde Hatabelle. When it was over Gail stood at the corral gate where Hatabelle was saddling his horse. "Jim won't come here," she reasoned. "He will know this is where they'll watch for him. I think he will try for Rand's place, or Red Pomeroy's."

"A long walk for him," Hatabelle said. "Especially on so dark a night."

"Perhaps it's luck there is no moon," Gail murmured. She shook her head, saying, "I shouldn't have fed Ernie Wade. I felt like a traitor, watching him eat while Jim Maiben goes hungry. And Jim may be wounded, for all we know."

As Hatabelle climbed into saddle, she said, "Tell them not to believe Bart Volpert's lies. Explain that it's some sort of frame-up between Volpert and Sheriff Bishop. Perhaps they'll help you look for him."

"Not Alamo," Hatabelle said. "His wife doesn't want him out of her sight since he was shot at. She's worried half sick for fear he'll be killed."

"Then ask Red Pomeroy. Red certainly has no love for Volpert who took his girl away from him. Ask Red to look for Jim, then circle down to Wade's place and tell Burro Smith. He's Jim's friend."

Hatabelle smiled at her. "Anyone would think I was also."

"Well, it's a way of making up for your mistake, Clyde. The best way you'll ever have."

"Yes, it's the least I can do."

Gail watched him ride from the yard. Then, instead of going back to the house, she picked up her own bridle and went into the corral.

Eric Steffan, sitting on the stoop, wondered about that. And moments later, as Gail began saddling her horse, he called across the yard, "Where are you going, girl?"

"To look for Jim Maiben."

"No!" Steffan protested urgently. "That I will not have!"

"But he may be hurt," Gail said. "I just can't sit here waiting and doing nothing."

"I will not have you riding at night while men with guns are prowling around. You might be mistaken for Maiben. You might be shot."

With the habitual obedience of a daughter who had never defied her father, Gail asked, "Do you forbid me to go?"

"Yes," he said sternly. "Tonight I forbid you. If Maiben is not found by daylight then you can go."

Then, as Gail led her horse back into the corral, Steffan counselled, "Do not worry about him, girl. Jim Maiben is a man who can take care of himself."

"But he's afoot, and there are three of them hunting him," Gail said worriedly. "He hasn't a fair chance."

Afterward, sitting on the stoop with her father, she listened for the sound of distant shooting. . . .

CHAPTER SEVENTEEN

Jim Maiben became aware of pain. It throbbed in his temples with a racking intensity that was echoed by the rhythmic thudding of horses hoofs. Dust got into his mouth and nostrils. There was an intolerable pounding ache in his stomach, and a sense of whirling motion that made him dizzy. A hot thrust of nausea rose in his throat and gagged him.

Some time after that Maiben realized that he was on a horse, belly down across a saddle. The horse was trotting and the jolt of the saddle was a continuous clubbing against his stomach. He attempted to ease that jolting by changing position, but his hands and feet were tied securely. The pain in his head got worse. It became a throbbing pressure that pounded louder and louder until finally it exploded against his eardrums with a crash that deafened him.

There was a merciful silence then, and an

odd sensation of floating farther and farther away from reality. For a long time there was the silence, and the floating. On and on. Then the sense of sound returned to him and he was remotely aware of voices, and the ache in his head, and the nausea. He came close to consciousness, then floated away again.

Maiben had no memory of vomiting, but the smell of it was in his nostrils. That and the acrid dust. He was sick again, and retched violently. Some time after that he felt himself being lifted off the horse, and heard Sid Bishop say, "He's still alive."

That didn't make sense to Maiben. Opening his eyes he couldn't focus them properly. He seemed to be lying on a bunk in a dimly lighted room of some sort. A queer, cavelike room. . . .

From somewhere beyond his vision Bart Volpert said, "I'll be back by noon. Maybe sooner. You keep a close watch, and don't do no shooting unless you have to. Sound carries a long ways in these canyons and we got to keep it quiet."

Presently Maiben heard a horse move off at a trot. Where, he wondered, was Volpert going?

And what about Grace?

What had happened to her?

Maybe that's where Volpert was going now. To horsewhip Grace. Maiben hunched up on an elbow, bracing himself against the multiple aches this motion brought. Rolling over, he saw Sid Bishop come through a doorway. The sheriff picked up a lantern and adjusted its wick and muttered, "Globe needs cleaning."

"He's going to whip Grace," Maiben announced thickly. "He'll use the buggy whip on her again. Got to stop him."

"What you blabbing about?" Bishop demanded. "What'd you say about Grace?"

Sid looked ghoulish, standing there with the lantern in his hands. The light came up into his face in an odd way, exaggerating the under side of his chin and nostrils, giving him a fiendish look.

"What did you say?" he asked again.

Maiben tried to remember what it was he wanted to tell Bishop. Something about Grace. But he couldn't recall what it was . . .

"So you finally woke up," Sid reflected. "Didn't think you would."

Maiben couldn't understand that. He lay back, shielding his eyes with an arm, and tried to guess what Bishop meant. He asked, "Where am I?" and heard Sid say something about a hide-out canyon, but he felt too drowsy to listen. . . .

When Maiben awoke again it was daylight and Bishop sat at a rude table drinking coffee. Maiben peered about the room, observing that the back and sides were of rock, with a log wall at the front. A dugout, he guessed, somewhere in Volpert's secret canyon. His head was clear again.

"You want some coffee?" Bishop asked.

Maiben nodded. He sat up, grimacing at the soreness of his stomach muscles. He lifted a hand to his temple and fingered a blood-crusted furrow that was sore to his touch.

"Volpert missed killing you again," Bishop said, watching him.

He chuckled, and scratched his whisker-bristled chin thoughtfully as he peered at Maiben's blood-stained temple. "It beats hell how bullets bounce off you. Never saw the beat of it."

"The dame had her arms around me," Maiben said. "She protects me."

"Dame? What dame?" Bishop demanded.

"Lady Luck. She likes me, on account of I'm kind to frogs."

"Frogs?" Bishop inquired, eying him suspiciously.

Maiben nodded, very solemn about this. "After Hatabelle's settlers damned off the water from the South Fork of Canteen

Creek whole generations of frogs grew up without learning to swim."

"What difference would that make to Lady Luck?" Sid asked in the gentle voice of a man pacifying a harmless idiot.

"She liked the way I saved those frogs' lives."

Bishop stared at him. "You saved them?"

Maiben nodded.

"How?"

"Well, I rounded up all the young ones and drove them to North Fork where they could learn to swim. Otherwise, if a flash flood had hit Canteen Creek they'd have drowned, sure as hell."

"You out of your mind?" Bishop demanded, looking horrified.

He kept staring at Maiben; he said, "That bullet must've addled your brain."

"Well, I feel a trifle queer for a fact," Maiben admitted, retaining a strict solemnity. "Reckon I'd better drink some coffee."

He got to his feet and stood there for a moment, feeling dizzy and light-headed. It was an effort to walk straight as he went to the stove. The coffeepot was almost full. He poured himself a cup and returned to the bunk.

Why, he wondered, hadn't Volpert finished him off at Spade?

There had been nothing to stop him, unless he didn't want to do it in front of Grace. But that scarcely seemed a logical reason. Volpert had her so afraid of him that she wouldn't dare to tell about a murder. He wondered if Grace knew about the calf stealing and supposed she didn't.

The strong coffee made a welcome warmth inside him. It banished the queer feeling that he was only half awake, and it revived him physically. Remembering what Grace had told him, Maiben gave Bishop a calculating appraisal. It seemed fantastic that any man would allow his daughter to be treated as Grace had been, regardless of the consequences to himself. That girl was being murdered by inches; day in and day out, month after month, she was being destroyed as surely as if Volpert had fired a bullet into her brain on their wedding day. He didn't understand Bishop.

"So you made your girl marry Bart Volpert." Maiben said.

"Did Grace tell you that?"

Maiben nodded.

"What else did she tell you?" Bishop demanded suspiciously.

"Well, she told me the reason she had to marry Volpert. But I still don't see why you made her do it."

Bishop shook his head. Gravely, in the defensive way of a man with a guilty conscience, he said, "Bart fixed that. He fixes every damned thing he puts his mind to any way he wants it."

"How'd he fix it?"

"By finding out I was wanted in Texas. He threatened to tell about it unless Grace married him."

"That's no excuse," Maiben muttered.

"What else could I do?"

"You could've killed Volpert."

Bishop shook his head again. "Bart fixed that also. He deposited a sealed letter at the bank, telling about the trouble I got into in Texas. He wrote on the envelope that it wasn't to be opened except in case of his death. I was helpless."

Bishop shrugged. "At first I thought about robbing the bank, to get hold of that paper. But I had no way of knowing just where George Jessop kept such things. Then I asked George if he had such an envelope and he said yes. I guess George got suspicious about me. That was right after Bart bought out Ike Fenton so cheap. George asked me if the envelope contained Volpert's will, leaving Fenton's place to me."

So that was why Jessop had been suspicious. George might have suspected Volpert

230

also, but he had died before he could tell the rest of it. . . .

"Now Volpert owns you, body and soul," Maiben reflected.

Sid didn't like that. He said harshly, "A man does what he has to do."

"A man?" Maiben scoffed.

Anger flared in Bishop's eyes. "Don't get sassy!" he warned. "Bart wants you kept alive for a spell, but that don't stop me from kicking your teeth out! And I will if I have to!"

Maiben thought about that as he finished his coffee. What reason could Volpert have for keeping him alive at all?

He asked, "What's Bart got up his sleeve?"

Bishop chuckled, and now his benevolent smile returned. "More tricks than you could shake a stick at. I ain't saying I've got any love for him, but you've got to give the devil his due. Bart figures everything out in advance. He looks ahead. Not just tomorrow, or next week, or next year. But way out yonder. Shouldn't wonder if he'd be the biggest man in Arizona Territory one of these days. Governor, even."

"Why did he tote me here instead of finishing me off at Spade last night?" Maiben asked.

"That's what I mean by him looking

ahead like he does," Bishop explained. "Most men would've chopped you down right then and there. Especially if they was as mad as Bart was when he found you pumping Grace for family secrets. Any other man would've killed you deader'n hell. But not Bart. Soon as he found out that his bullet had just stunned you, he saw how a live jailbird could be made into a first-class scapegoat."

"How?"

"Well, Bart has got his eye on that North Fork land. He's been throwing a scarce into those folks, now and then, just to make them spooky. He pulled another one man raid there last night. A shootup raid that folks will blame on you."

"Why should they blame it on me?"

Bishop laughed, enjoying this; he asked, "Where's your hat?"

When Maiben shrugged, Sid said, "I'll tell you where it is. Or leastwise where it was this morning until it was found. At North Fork."

"So that's where Volpert went," Maiben mused, baffled at the scope of his scheming.

"And that ain't all," Bishop announced braggingly. "Tonight there'll be another shootup raid, this one at Roman Six, which will also be blamed on you."

That announcement astonished Maiben. "What good will that do Volpert?"

"Plenty, if old Steffan should happen to get shot again. The girl would sell out cheap, wouldn't she? And so will others. Even after you're found dead they'll be afraid of your calf thief pardners."

That explanation shocked Jim Maiben. Even now, knowing Volpert's insatiable greed, it seemed fantastic that one man should attempt to take over a whole range single-handed. Volpert had no crew of hired gunhawks. All he had for help was an obedient sheriff. . . .

"So Volpert intends to take over the whole basin, including North Fork," Maiben mused, scarcely able to believe it.

Bishop nodded. He spread his palms in an expansive gesture. "Bart and I will run this whole shebang one of these days. Think what it will mean, with all that range in one big ranch. Alamo Rand's place will be headquarters, on account of being about in the middle. We'll have a crew to do the riding while me and Bart take our ease. Spade and them other places will be line-camps, and we'll import some Mex farmers to sharecrop the North Fork flats."

"You won't get away with it," Maiben

argued. "Nobody can bite off that big a chunk without getting caught."

Bishop laughed at him. "Did they catch us when Fenton's shack was burned? Or when Steffan was wounded? Or when Wade sold out for a dime on the dollar? Hell no. And it'll be the same with them other places. A few stubborn ones may have to be chopped down. But it can be blamed on you and your thieving pardners. And it will be."

That announcement convinced Jim Maiben. Here, he understood, was a man with no normal sense of right or wrong. Trapped by Volpert because of a past crime, he had turned into a tool dedicated to the ruin of a whole region; an obedient, unquestioning tool that had already sacrificed his own daughter on the altar of Volpert's greed.

And tonight Eric Steffan was to be the victim. . . .

Abruptly now came the realization that Gail would be endangered by a raid at Roman Six. The thought sickened Maiben. It roused an overwhelming dread that was stronger, somehow, than his own need for survival. Thinking back to last night, Maiben recalled Volpert's announcement that he would return by noon. Perhaps sooner. Maiben peered out the doorway; attempting to guess the hour. Not more than nine or ten o'clock, he judged, which meant he might have another hour alone with Bishop. He thought, one hour to make a getaway, to save Steffan.

But how could he accomplish it?

Sid had a six-shooter and was fully capable of using it against an unarmed prisoner. Thinking that Sid might have brought his rifle inside, Maiben gave the dugout a surreptitious survey, and saw no sign of the Winchester. Or anything else that could be used for a weapon to aid his cause.

For several minutes Maiben put his mind to devising some plan, some trickery that would give him a chance to escape. Gail and her father should be warned; they should be sent to town before dark and remain there until Volpert was caught or killed. But first he had to get out of here. . . .

Bishop, he thought, was like Volpert had been yesterday at the canyon's entrance: wholly confident. Perhaps, if he could get close enough to the sheriff, he might use the same tactics on him. So thinking, Maiben got up and walked casually toward the doorway, intending to turn on Bishop as he came abreast of him. But Sid ordered suspiciously, "Stay away from that door," and dropped his right hand to holster.

"Well, you want me to do it inside?" Maiben asked sharply.

"What you got to do?"

Maiben held up one finger.

"Do it in the corner over there," Sid directed. "You can't go outside alone, and I don't feel like tromping around. All this night riding gets me down."

When Maiben came back from the corner he changed his course so that he passed on the other side of the table.

"Where you heading for now?" Bishop demanded angrily.

"Just getting another cup of coffee, is all."

Going to the stove Maiben lifted the coffeepot and asked, "You want another?"

Bishop nodded, and held up his cup to be filled.

Maiben came over to the table and tilted the pot as if to pour. But instead he sluiced its contents into Bishop's face and lunging at the same instant, tried to tie Sid up so that he couldn't draw his gun. But Bishop, half blinded and yelping profanely, evaded that first rush, and now Maiben had to grab his right arm as the gun cleared leather.

Bishop wheeled, attempting to pull free. He clouted Maiben with his left fist and snarled pantingly, "Let go, or I'll kill you!"

But Maiben hung on, forcing the gun's

snout away from him. He got a leg lock on Bishop and lost it as Bishop pounded him with his left hand. Sid kept stabbing at the raw wound on Maiben's temple; kept clawing at his eyes. Maiben pressed his face against Bishop's shoulder and getting his teeth into the muscle, heard Sid's gusty yelping.

"You goddamn bulldog!" Bishop accused, using his head to butt Maiben's face away from his shoulder.

Maiben got another leg lock on Bishop and tried to throw him, but Sid backed against the table. Using it for support, Bishop carried Maiben over the table top with him. They went down together, with Maiben underneath, grunting in agony as Sid's weight smashed against his sore stomach. Maiben fought for wind and had trouble getting breath back into his lungs. But he clung to Bishop's arms and came up off the floor with him.

Bishop rammed Maiben against the dugout's rear wall. He pulled back and was on the point of repeating the performance when Maiben drove a knee into Bishop's crotch.

Sid loosed a whimpering curse, and Maiben thought exultantly, One more like that and he'll have to drop the gun!

But hurt as he was, Bishop wheeled away, carrying Maiben with him. And at this instant, as they floundered in the middle of the room, Maiben saw Bart Volpert rush through the doorway and knew dismally that time had run out on him.

"Pull away from him, Sid!" Volpert shouted as he ran toward them.

There was no strength in Bishop now. Maiben swung him around at will, using him for a human shield. Volpert kept circling, kept watching for a chance to fire without hitting Bishop. Stepping in close, he slashed at Maiben's head with the barrel of his gun. Maiben ducked and the barrel struck Bishop's skull with a sickening crunch that was like the sound of a bone breaking. As Bishop collapsed, Maiben snatched at Sid's gun and was knocked aside by Volpert who snarled, "You're done, Maiben! All done!"

Exhausted and panting, and soaked with sweat, Maiben understood that this was so. Nothing he could say or do would alter the outcome now. He was finished, Bishop had opened the wound on his temple so that blood dribbled into his right eye; he knuckled the blood away and waited for Volpert to shoot, and wondered why he didn't. Then he remembered what Bart had told Sid about not shooting unless he had to, because of the noise. Volpert, he supposed, was afraid of attracting attention to his secret canyon. Perhaps he intended to pistol-whip him to death, as he had Bishop. That wouldn't make much noise.

Maiben thought, A cautious, self-winding son!

With the black boots of futility tromping him, he said rankly, "You're what I called you three years ago, Volpert. Owning three ranches hasn't changed that. All the land in Rampage Basin wouldn't change it. You'd still be a goddamn gutless coward."

Volpert thumbed back the hammer of his gun. His muddy eyes were brighter now than Maiben had ever seen them; almost amber. "A coward who stands to own every place in the Barricade Hills," he bragged, "including yours."

His dribbling laughter was like a giggle as he said, "I knew you'd come back hunting trouble soon as they opened the penitentiary gates. And I made my plans accordingly. It was getting to where I needed a scapegoat, Maiben, and you got back just in time."

Then an odd thing happened. A shadow flitted across the floor and as Volpert glanced down at it, Clyde Hatabelle called from the doorway, "I've got you covered, Bart!"

Volpert went rigid, as if paralyzed beyond the power of movement. "Don't shoot!" he pleaded in a quavering, falsetto voice. "Don't shoot me, Clyde!"

He still had a gun in his hand. But now he wilted visibly. Perspiration greased his pock-pitted face and his whole body slumped so that he stood in knee-sprung weakness. Turning to look over his shoulder at Hatabelle, he asked meekly, "Why me, Clyde? Why cover me? Maiben is the one you're after."

"No," Hatabelle said, and his voice was also high-pitched with excitement. "I heard what you said about owning every ranch in the hills."

Maiben had stepped around Volpert. Now he snatched the gun from Volpert's hand and said, "Here's where you get your needings."

Holstering the gun, Maiben grasped Volpert's shoulder and yanked him around and hit him in the face. "That's for the shack burning deal," he muttered, and seeing Volpert go down, was surprised that the blow had felled him."

"You've knocked him out," Hatabelle blurted with frank admiration. "One blow, and you knocked him cold."

Maiben shrugged, said, "I didn't intend to

240

hit him that hard. I wanted to punish him for what he did to Grace."

Then, glimpsing Volpert's darting grab toward Bishop's gun on the floor, Maiben understood Bart's sly strategy.

It was a close thing. Maiben fired as Volpert tilted the gun up. This first shot was instinctive. Defensive. But because the need for vengeance had been in him so long, Maiben fired again and again, driving bullets into the pock-pitted face until it became a pulpy, blood-smeared mask, grotesque and lifeless.

Clyde Hatabelle went hastily outside and was sick. Maiben ejected the spent shells from his gun and reloaded it. Remembering his promise to the locker-room clerk at Yuma, he thought, Now there's a notch on my gun.

Hatabelle came to the doorway and asked, "Is Bishop dead, too?"

Maiben nodded and walked outside. He asked, "How'd you happen to find your way here?"

"Saw Volpert ride through what looked like a wall of rock," Hatabelle explained. "I thought at first it was you, until I remembered that a North Fork settler brought your hat to Roman Six this morning."

"Another of Volpert's tricks," Maiben said.

"I was to be his scapegoat."

Hatabelle nodded. "That's how we figured it."

"We?"

"The Steffans, and Red Pomeroy. We were having breakfast when Hank Pelky brought news of the North Fork raid. Red and I looked for you most of last night, along with Burro Smith. We knew you were afoot and needing help."

"How'd you know that?"

"Ernie Wade stopped by for supper. He told us what was going on. So I saddled up and went looking for you, along with Red and Burro."

"You did that — last night?" Maiben demanded. "Hours before you heard what Volpert said about taking over the range?"

Hatabelle nodded. "It was little enough, considering the mistake I'd made."

Maiben shrugged and started toward a saddled horse. Then abruptly realizing how much he owed this land agent he had once hated, he said, "I'm much obliged for you saving me like you did. I was a gone goose for sure this time."

That seemed to embarrass Hatabelle. He shook his head. "It's bothered me a lot, thinking that I might have made a mistake three years ago. Even when Gail Steffan

242

guessed the truth about Volpert, I couldn't believe he was the man I saw leaving Fenton's place. But I know it now."

"Well, this deal makes it even," Maiben said. "More than even."

He went to Volpert's horse and mounted, saying, "I'll let you take care of the rest of it. I feel six years older'n God."

Hatabelle nodded agreement to that. He said, "If you see Red Pomeroy send him up here. And be careful about the others. Especially toward Roman Six. Ernie Wade is hunting you. He's half out of his mind. Says Dulcie told him you had put a hex on her."

Maiben grinned. "She means I sicked Burro Smith onto her," he mused. "Burro treated her like the tart she is."

"Keep your eyes peeled for Wade over toward Roman Six," Hatabelle warned again.

"Not going that way."

Hatabelle showed his surprise by asking, "Then where are you going?"

Maiben shrugged. "The Tinajas Altas, maybe. Or up on the Strip. Some place where a cowpoke can get a job riding for wages."

He was thinking about that as he rode out of the canyon. It seemed odd for a man to be traveling with no set destination. But that was how it would be for him from now on. A drifter with no more home than a tumbleweed.

Hearing a horse clatter over loose rock, Maiben pulled in behind a manzanita thicket and drew his gun. Someone was coming off a ledge just ahead of him. In the moment while he waited, Maiben remembered Hatabelle's warning and hoped this wasn't a North Fork settler wanting a shot at him. It would be too bad if he had to kill one of those plow jockeys in self-defense, after the frame-up he had escaped.

Then, as the rider came into view, Maiben called, "Hi, Red!"

Pomeroy grinned at him and said, "Thought you was afoot."

"Stole a horse," Maiben said.

While they shaped up cigarettes and smoked them, he told Pomeroy about Grace, and what had happened in the canyon. "She's a widow woman now, and an orphan to boot. She's not as pretty as she was three years ago, Red. But she feels the same toward you as she did then. The poor girl has been through hell."

"I'll make it up to her," Red said soberly. "By God I'm sorry you killed Volpert. Any man that would horsewhip Grace should've had his heart cut out by a dull knife. Shooting was too damned good for that bastard for my money."

"Yeah," Maiben agreed. "I felt the same way. But I didn't have much choice." Then he added, "Clyde Hatabelle wants you to come up and help him pack the bodies out. It's the first canyon back there by that manzanita. You'll have to look —"

"Hell with the bodies," Pomeroy said impatiently. "I'm going to get Grace."

Whereupon he kicked his horse into a lope and rode northward.

Maiben smiled. He thought, It will be all right for her now. Grace would probably never forgive him for causing her father's death. Even if she learned that he hadn't actually killed Bishop she would blame him for it. But that didn't matter. Nothing mattered, except getting out of this damned country and forgetting the whole sorry mess.

Nearing Spanish Spring Maiben remembered his first meeting with Gail Steffan. How queenlike she had looked standing there in the fading sunlight. Gail had called him a saddletramp that day, and wiped off her lips as if his kiss had tainted them. But she had bandaged his wound, and washed his blood-stained shirt, regardless. And she had taken his word about the shack burning. Comparing her calm acceptance with the disbelief of all the others, Maiben felt an insistent urge to see Gail again. Perhaps he could contrive a farewell kiss. A sort of token kiss for luck. That would complete the circle: a stolen kiss the day he arrived in the Barricade Hills and another one the day he left.

Maiben grinned, recalling the riddle of her response. Gail, he supposed, was as astonished that day as he had been. But she had never acted as if she regretted it. The thought came to him that he might have a chance with her, now that his name had been cleared.

Hell, he had killed the sneaky son who'd wounded her father, hadn't he?

Gail would appreciate that. She might even think it was important enough to change her mind about marrying Clyde.

But even as that possibility tempted him, Maiben shook his head. Gail was promised to Hatabelle, and Hatabelle had saved his life. A man couldn't forget a thing like that. . . .

Maiben was skirting a prowlike bulge in the divide when he glimpsed Ernie Wade directly ahead of him. Ernie pulled up at once; he blurted, "You dirty bastard!" and grabbed for his gun.

"No, Ernie!" Maiben shouted. "Wait!"

But Ernie wasn't waiting. He fired in such frenzied haste that the bullet kicked up dust in front of Maiben's horse. His gun was blasting again as Maiben fired.

Wade's second bullet whanged close to Maiben's head. Maiben cursed, and fired again, then watched Wade tip over. As the startled horse wheeled in a pivoting turn, Ernie fell headlong and lay still.

Maiben rode over to him and dismounted. Seeing the blue-rimmed hole in Ernie's forehead he felt an odd mixture of regret and anger and futility. "You poor fool," he muttered, and despised Dulcie Todd for discarding this man who'd been her husband. He picked up Ernie's hat and gently placed it over his slack-jawed face, and whispered, "You poor damned fool."

Afterward, dropping down to the hoof-pocked seep at Spanish Spring, Maiben felt a depressing sense of kinship for the man he had killed. They had both lost their ranches, and both been discarded by a swivel-hipped flirt with no more morals than a female rabbit.

Dismounting at the spring he lay down in the mud, liking its dampness against his sore belly as he drank. It occurred to him that

247

this was like it had been that other day. He smiled, remembering how the impulse to kiss Gail Steffan had overwhelmed him. It had seemed the natural thing to do; natural as breathing. And it seemed like a long time ago, so much had happened since then. He hadn't known about the sale of his ranch, or George Jessop's death, or Dulcie Todd's marriage, or that a sorrel-haired woman would bewitch him. He had been so filled with hatred that nothing else mattered: the hatred Father Michael had told him was his personal prison.

The old priest had been right about that. "I'll tell him so if I ever get out Yuma way again," Maiben mused.

There was no hatred in Maiben now. He was free of it; free as a migratory bird. But freedom didn't seem to have much meaning. He felt old and tired and empty. Life played odd tricks on a man, pushing him every which way. Sometimes up so high he felt tall as a windmill, then down to where he was lower than snake sign in a wheelrut.

Aware of the mucky dampness soaking through his shirt, Maiben thought, Which is how I am now.

He was still lying there when he heard sound above him.

Rearing up instantly and clawing for his

gun, Maiben stared at Gail Steffan who stood in a cleft of rock above the spring. Her oval face — the battered felt hat with tawny hair showing below it — everything about this moment seemed wholly familiar to Jim Maiben. It was as if a clock had been turned back. For a moment of sheer bafflement he wondered if he was dreaming; if he was just remembering this from that other time. . . .

Then she called down, "Jim, are you all right?"

Maiben nodded, not speaking as he watched her come toward him with a led horse behind her.

She said, "I heard shots and was worried. Have you seen Clyde?"

Maiben nodded again, thinking it was Clyde she was fretting about. But she said, "I was afraid some of the North Fork settlers might shoot at you. There's a dozen of them in the hills today. I tried to convince them that it wasn't you who shot up the settlement last night. But they wouldn't believe me because of the hat Volpert left for a clue."

"How did you know Volpert left it?" Maiben asked.

Gail shrugged. "Well, it seemed plain enough to me."

She came up to him and glanced at his mud-smeared shirt and said, "You look just like you did the first time I saw you." Then she peered at the blood-crusted wound on his temple and added, "Except for that."

"Think it needs disinfecting?" Maiben inquired.

"Yes, and you need a clean shirt. Also a shave."

Something in the way she looked at him now put a thrusting urge in Maiben; an impulse so strong that he could scarcely resist it. She looked, by God, like a woman who wanted to be kissed!

There was this moment when he almost reached out for her; this timeless interval when she seemed to be expecting him to take her in his arms. But he couldn't quite forget that she belonged to Clyde Hatabelle who had saved his life.

Maiben took out his Durham sack, glanced at its moisture-sogged condition, and tossed it away. He said, "Hatabelle saved my bacon today. Volpert had me all set for shooting when Clyde showed up."

"Good for Clyde!" Gail exclaimed, wholly pleased. Then she added teasingly, "Saved by a gentle Annie."

Maiben accepted that with a self-mocking smile. He said, "Well, Clyde will get his reward."

"What reward?"

"You."

That seemed to surprise her, for she asked, "Did Clyde tell you that?"

"Why, no. But didn't you say you were going to marry him?"

Gail shook her head. "I told you he asked me to marry him, is all."

Jim Maiben peered at her in squint-eyed astonishment. "You mean Hatabelle isn't planning to marry you?"

"Not unless he's intending to become a bigamist," Gail said smilingly. "Clyde is engaged to Effie Jessop."

In the moment it took Maiben to absorb that information, Gail said, "Dad wants you for a partner, Jim. He doesn't feel right about you losing the place as you did, and anyway, there's more work than one man can do. Even when he's able to ride again, Dad couldn't possibly take care of the work he has planned."

Maiben wasn't interested in that part of it. He asked, "Is there any other reason why I should go back to Roman Six?"

Color crept into Gail's cheeks as she considered his question for a long moment. She said, "Well, your hat is there."

Then, dropping all pretense, she asked,

"Oh, Jim — must I tell you how it is with me? How it's been since that first kiss!"

She moved into the circle of his arms and snuggled against his mud-smeared chest. She said, with the frank urgency of a woman in love, "Kiss me, Jim. Please kiss me."

And he did.

ABOUT THE AUTHOR

Leslie Ernenwein was born in Oneida, New York. He began his newspaper career as a telegraph editor, but at eighteen went West where he rambled from Montana to Mexico, working as a cowboy and then as a freelance writer. In the mid 1930s he went back East to work for the *Schenectady Sun.* In 1938 he got a reporting position with the *Tucson Daily Citizen* and moved to Tucson permanently. Later that year he began writing Western fiction for pulp magazines, becoming a regular contributor to *Dime Western* and *Star Western.* His first Western novel, *Gunsmoke Galoot,* appeared in 1941, and was quickly followed by *Kinkade of Red Butte* and *Boss of Panamint* in 1942. In addition to publishing novels regularly, Ernenwein continued to contribute heavily to the magazine market, both Western fiction and factual articles. Among his finest work in the 1940s are *Rebels Ride Proudly* (1947)

253

and *Rebel Yell* (1948), both dealing with the dislocations caused by the War Between the States. In the 1950s Ernenwein wrote primarily for original paperback publishers of Western fiction because the pay was better. *High Gun* in 1956, published by Fawcett Gold Medal, won a Spur Award from the Western Writers of America, the first original paperback Western to do so. That same year, since the pulp magazine market had all but vanished, Ernenwein returned to working for the *Tucson Daily Citizen*, this time as a columnist. Ernenwein's Western fiction may be broadly characterized as moral allegories, light against darkness, and at the center is a protagonist determined to fight against injustice before he is destroyed by it. *Bullet Barricade* (1955), perhaps his most notable novel from the 1950s, best articulates his vision of how the life of man is not governed by a fate over which he has no control, even though life itself may seem like a never-ending contest against moral evil.

We hope you have enjoyed this Large Print book. Other Thorndike, Wheeler, and Chivers Press Large Print books are available at your library or directly from the publishers.

For information about current and upcoming titles, please call or write, without obligation, to:

Publisher
Thorndike Press
295 Kennedy Memorial Drive
Waterville, ME 04901
Tel. (800) 223-1244

or visit our Web site at:

http://gale.cengage.com/thorndike

OR

Chivers Large Print
published by BBC Audiobooks Ltd
St James House, The Square
Lower Bristol Road
Bath BA2 3SB
England
Tel. +44(0) 800 136919
email: bbcaudiobooks@bbc.co.uk
www.bbcaudiobooks.co.uk

All our Large Print titles are designed for easy reading, and all our books are made to last.